Dav

Davy Byrnes Stories

The six prize-winning stories from the
2009 Davy Byrnes Irish Writing Award
as selected by Richard Ford

The Stinging Fly

A Stinging Fly Press Book

Davy Byrnes Stories first published December 2009.

Set in Palatino
Printed by Betaprint, Dublin

© Individual Authors 2009

ISBN 978-1-906539-11-5

The Stinging Fly Press
PO Box 6016
Dublin 8
www.stingingfly.org

The Stinging Fly Press gratefully acknowledges funding support from
The Arts Council/An Chomhairle Ealaíon and Dublin City Council.

Contents

The Davy Byrnes Irish Writing Award is sponsored by Davy Byrnes of Duke Street, Dublin 2. It is Ireland's biggest competition for a single short story and it aims to honour the great tradition of short story writing in Ireland and to encourage and reward excellence among current practitioners of the form. The competition was first held in 2004 as part of the Bloomsday Centenary celebrations organised by the James Joyce Centre.

Anne Enright won the 2004 Award for her story 'Honey'. The other short-listed writers were Kevin Barry, Linda Dennard, Philip Ó Ceallaigh, Breda Wall Ryan and Michael West.

The 2009 Award was organised by The Stinging Fly in association with The Irish Times. More than eight hundred entries were received by the February 2nd deadline. All of the stories were first read anonymously by a panel of readers with a final selection of thirty going on to be read by Richard Ford.

Judge's Report

Richard Ford

I'VE ALWAYS RESISTED NOTIONS of national literature, and the suggestion that there's a distinctive Irish short story and voice, or a distinctive American one, or a Bulgarian one or a Somali one. Yes, okay, there *may* be detectable differences. But literature's great opportunity is, in part, to make all these tongues speak a universal language that subordinates frail nation-state concerns in favor of more basic human ones which require champions. I still doggedly believe that, and have taken that premise to the business of reading these Davy Byrnes stories this spring. I wasn't trying to find the *most Irish story* in the bunch, but rather to find what seemed to be the most excellent one. Of course the thirty stories I read represented the cream of a fairly large crop of hundreds of entrants; and to submit a story one needed to demonstrate some elementary form of Irishness (what that could be I don't know and don't want to know—for reasons of indelicacy). But I must say that reading these thirty stories has left me with the unexpected impression that your regulation-grade Irish man or woman might just be able to write a pretty decent short story in his or her sleep.

It's possible that there may be an 'experimental movement' in current Irish story writing, but it wasn't in evidence in these stories—which may have more to do with the early winnowing out process before I got my thirty. The progress of the narratives wasn't always lock-step chronological, and some were fragmented and minimal and elliptical; but they didn't seem to want to subvert standard notions of time's passage, either in the story or out in the world. The stories, indeed, seemed to accept that the world was out there being problematical, and that a story was a special place that mimicked the world by the use of language, but meant to direct us back to that world with a heightened awareness.

Likewise, characters in these stories made sense pretty much the way people do in the streets of Dublin (i.e. doggedly, colorfully, elliptically, profanely, sometimes eloquently). Thus the formal feature of human 'character' itself wasn't in dispute—except in moral-ethical, but not ontological ways.

Intimate life—between lovers, between friends, among families—was the recurrent subject matter. And houses in streets, the interiors of automobiles, bed (of course), the recognizable sea-side, foreign countries whose names we know were mostly used as life's plausible settings. Most of the stories seem to think that drama was to be found in unhappy circumstances—families that didn't work, loves that didn't flourish, age that wouldn't stop for a breather, the approach of the grim reaper, him/herself. And most stories didn't turn out altogether happily at their ends. I could've done with a few more laughs, to tell the truth. Maybe a few gay Irishmen. A few Irish citizens of color. If you're writing about the actual world, well… they're in there, too.

There wasn't *a lot* of the *Irish being Irish* in these stories (of course there was some, inescapably). And especially among the best of the stories a reader might not know—or if he did he didn't care—that Ireland was even the setting when it was. I was happy about this, although I can't quite say why.

Language was most often the shining beauty in these stories—as opposed to narrative structure, plottedness (of which there was precious little), or other fictive formalities. To my American ear, narrators and characters in these stories seemed to enjoy expressing themselves, seemed to like the feel of words in their virtual mouths, seemed to think that important life was largely lived in language—in what we say to each other, about each other, remember of each other, in how we love, detest, ignore, demean and relish. In that way language was the window to the world, but also the pane that mediates and colors it, and on occasion it was the view itself. Here is where I found the most pleasure in these thirty stories, and it was the virtue that drew me exuberantly back to reading each day. For writers—who inevitably see the world, as Pritchett said, from across a frontier—words are our medium, our transit, and our precious subject. These stories all seemed generously to share that conviction, and to want to make the most—not the least—of its possibilities.

This report first appeared in The Irish Times *on Saturday June 6th, 2009.*
© Richard Ford 2009

Foster

Claire Keegan

Award Citation

'Foster' puts on display an imposing array of formal beauties at the service of a deep and profound talent. It tells a conceivably simple story—a young child given up to grieving foster parents and then woefully wrested home again. Claire Keegan makes the reader sure that there are no simple stories, and that art is essential to life. In lifting a homely rural existence to our moral notice, she brings a thrilling synaesthetic instinct for the unexpected right word, and exhibits patient attention to life's vast consequence and finality. She knows when to linger and never does so without profit, and indeed is never timid about saying more when less would be less. In this way she is a generous writer, always urging her sentences onward, adventurously extending our understanding, upping the ante, never obscuring or taking shelter in what can't be known. Yet sparkling talent aside, this is by no means a gaudy story—but a rather muted and decorous one entrusted to the voice of a child infused with the imagination of a seer. And yet to read it word upon word (as one must) is to experience a high-wire act of uncommon narrative virtuosity.

—Richard Ford

Author's note:

The story began with the image of the girl's hand reaching over the water. That stayed in the back of my mind for a long time. And then I started thinking about the well we used at home. It wasn't on our land but down from us in a field called Byrne's Lawn. Remembering how it felt to go down there to fetch water, I made a start. Then I was given a deadline, switched and finished another story. Winter came and I went for a walk on the strand in Wexford with a friend of mine. There were two lights on the water when we came up across the dunes. By the time we were leaving, he noticed three. I went back to the story in the new year, wrote the walk into the text and found the character of Kinsella. Maybe I wanted to write about a man who has lost his son. I knew little except that it needed to be written from a child's point of view and, later, that it would have to take place in summer. At no point in the writing of the story did I have clear feelings about where the story was going much less how it would conclude.

—*Claire Keegan*

1

EARLY ON A SUNDAY, after first Mass in Clonegal, my father, instead of taking me home, drives deep into Wexford towards the coast where my mother's people came from. It is a hot day, bright, with patches of shade and greenish, sudden light along the road. We pass through the village of Shillelagh where my father lost our red Shorthorn in a game of forty-five, and on past the mart in Carnew where the man who won the heifer sold her shortly afterwards. My father throws his hat on the passenger seat, winds down the window, and smokes. I shake the plaits out of my hair and lie flat on the back seat, looking up through the rear window. In places there's a bare, blue sky. In places the blue sky is chalked over with clouds, but mostly it is a heady mixture of sky and trees scratched over by ESB wires across which, every now and then, small, brownish flocks of vanishing birds race.

I wonder what it will be like, this place belonging to the Kinsellas. I see a tall woman standing over me, making me drink milk still hot from the cow. I see another, less likely version of her in an apron, pouring pancake batter onto a frying pan, asking would I like another, the way my mother sometimes does when she is in good humour. The man will be her size. He will take me to town on the tractor and buy me red lemonade and crisps. Or he'll make me clean out sheds and pick stones and pull ragweed and docks out of the fields. I see him pulling what I hope will be a fifty pence piece from his pocket but it turns out to be a handkerchief. I wonder if they live in an old farmhouse or a new bungalow, whether they will have an outhouse or an indoor bathroom with a toilet and running water. I picture myself lying in a dark bedroom with other girls, saying things we won't repeat when morning comes.

An age, it seems, passes before the car slows and turns into a tarred, narrow lane, then a thrill as the wheels slam over the metal bars of a cattle grid. On either side, thick hedges are trimmed square. At the end of the lane there's a long, white house with trees whose limbs are trailing the ground.

'Da,' I say. 'The trees.'

'What about 'em?'

'They're sick,' I say.

'They're weeping willows,' he says, and clears his throat.

In the yard, tall, shiny panes reflect our coming. I see myself looking out from the back seat wild as a tinker's child with my hair all loose but my father, at the wheel, looks just like my father. A big, loose hound whose coat is littered with the shadows of the trees lets out a few rough, half-hearted barks, then sits on the step and looks back at the doorway where the man has come out to stand. He has a square body like the men my sisters sometimes draw, but his eyebrows are white, to match his hair. He looks nothing like my mother's people, who are all tall with long arms and I wonder if we have not come to the wrong house.

'Dan,' he says, and tightens himself. 'What way are you?'

'John,' Da says.

They stand, looking out over the yard for a moment and then they are talking rain: how little rain there is, how the fields need rain, how the priest in Kilmuckridge prayed for rain that very morning, how a summer like it was never before known. There is a pause during which my father spits and then the conversation turns to the price of cattle, the EEC, butter mountains, the cost of lime and sheep-dip. It is something I am used to, this way men have of not talking: they like to kick a divot out of the grass with a boot heel, to slap the roof of a car before it takes off, to spit, to sit with their legs wide apart, as though they do not care.

When the woman comes out, she pays no heed to the men. She is even taller than my mother with the same black hair but hers is cut tight like a helmet. She's wearing a printed blouse and brown, flared trousers. The car door is opened and I am taken out, and kissed. My face, being kissed, turns hot against hers.

'The last time I saw you, you were in the pram,' she says, and stands back, expecting an answer.

'The pram's broken.'

'What happened at all?'

'My brother used it for a wheelbarrow and the wheel fell off.'

She laughs and licks her thumb and wipes something off my face. I can feel her thumb, softer than my mother's, wiping whatever it is away. When she looks at my clothes, I see my thin, cotton dress, my dusty sandals through her eyes. There's a moment when neither one of us knows what to say. A queer, ripe breeze is crossing the yard.

'Come on in, a Leanbh.'

She leads me into the house. There's a moment of darkness in the hallway; when I hesitate, she hesitates with me. We walk through into the heat of the kitchen where I am told to sit down, to make myself at home. Under the smell of baking there's some disinfectant, some bleach. She lifts a rhubarb tart out of the oven and puts it on the bench to cool: syrup on the point of bubbling over, thin leaves of pastry baked into the crust. A cool draught from the door blows in but here it is hot and still and clean. Tall ox-eyed daisies are still as the tall glass of water they are standing in. There is no sign, anywhere, of a child.

'So how is your mammy keeping?'

'She won a tenner on the prize bonds.'

'She did not.'

'She did,' I say. 'We all had jelly and ice cream and she bought a new tube and a mending kit for the bicycle.'

'Well, wasn't that a treat.'

'It was,' I say, and feel, again, the steel teeth of the comb against my scalp earlier that morning, the strength of my mother's hands as she wove the plaits tight, her belly at my back, hard with the next baby. I think of the clean pants she packed in the suitcase, the letter, and what she must have written. Words had passed between them:

'How long should they keep her?'

'Can't they keep her as long as they like?'

'Is that what I'll say?'

'Say what you like. Isn't it what you always do.'

Now, the woman fills an enamel jug with milk.

'Your mother must be busy.'

'She's waiting for them to come and cut the hay.'

'Have ye not the hay cut?' she says. 'Aren't ye late?'

When the men come in from the yard, it grows momentarily dark, then brightens once again when they sit down.

'Well, Missus,' says Da, pulling out a chair.

'Dan,' she says, in a different voice.

'There's a scorcher of a day.'

''Tis hot, surely.' She turns her back to watch the kettle, waiting.

'Wouldn't the fields be glad of a sup of rain,' he says.

'Won't we have the rain for long enough.' She looks at the wall as though a picture is hanging there but there is no picture on that wall, just a big mahogany clock with two hands and a big copper pendulum, swinging.

'Wasn't it a great year for the hay all the same. Never saw the like of it,' says Da. 'The loft is full to capacity. I nearly split my head on the rafters pitching it in.'

I wonder why my father lies about the hay. He is given to lying about things that would be nice, if they were true. Somewhere, further off, someone has started up a chainsaw and it drones on like a big, stinging wasp for a while in the distance. I wish I was out there, working. I am unused to sitting still and do not know what to do with my hands. Part of me wants my father to leave me here while another part of me wants him to take me back, to what I know. I am in a spot where I can neither be what I always am nor turn into what I could be.

The kettle lets off steam and rumbles up to boiling point, its steel lid clapping. The presence of a black and white cat moves on the window ledge. On the floor, across the hard, clean tiles, the woman's shadow stretches, almost reaching my chair. Kinsella gets up and takes a stack of plates from the cupboard, opens a drawer and takes out knives and forks, teaspoons. He takes the lid off a jar of beetroot and puts it on a saucer with a little serving fork, leaves out sandwich spread and salad cream. My father watches closely as he does this. Already there's a bowl of tomatoes and onions, chopped fine, a fresh loaf, a block of red cheddar.

'And what way is Mary?' the woman says.

'Mary? She's coming near her time.' Da sits back, satisfied.

'I suppose the last babby is getting hardy?'

'Aye,' Da says. 'It's the feeding them that's the trouble. There's no appetite like a child's and, believe you me, this one is no different.'

'Ah, don't we all eat in spurts, the same as we grow,' says

the woman, as though this is something he should know.

'She'll ate but you can work her.'

Kinsella looks up. 'There'll be no need for any of that,' he says. 'The child will have no more to do than help Edna around the house.'

'We'll keep the child gladly,' the woman echoes. 'She's welcome here.'

'She'll ate ye out of house and home,' Da says, 'but I don't suppose there'll be a word about it this time twelve months.'

When we sit in at the table, Da reaches for the beetroot. He doesn't use the serving fork but pitches it onto the plate with his own. It stains the pink ham, bleeds. Tea is poured. There's a patchy silence as we eat, as our knives and forks break up what's on our plates. Then, after some time, the tart is cut. Cream falls over the hot pastry, into pools.

Now that my father has delivered me and eaten his fill, he is anxious to light his fag and get away. Always, it's the same: he never stays in any place long after he's eaten, not like my mother who would talk until it grew dark and light again. This, at least, is what my father says even though I have never known it to happen. With my mother it is all work: us, the butter-making, the dinners, the washing up and getting up and getting ready for Mass and school, weaning calves, and hiring men to plough and harrow the fields, stretching the money and setting the alarm. But this is a different type of house. Here there is room, and time to think. There may even be money to spare.

'I'd better hit the road,' Da says.

'What hurry is on you?' Kinsella says.

'The daylight is burning, and I've yet the spuds to spray.'

'There's no fear of blight these evenings,' the woman says, but she gets up anyway, and goes out the back door with a sharp knife. I want to go with her, to shake the clay off whatever she cuts and carry it back into the house. A type of silence climbs between the men while she is out.

'Give this to Mary,' she says, coming in. 'I'm snowed under with rhubarb, whatever kind of year it is.'

My father takes it from her but it is as awkward as the baby in his arms. A stalk falls to the floor and then another. He waits for her to pick it up, to hand it to him. She waits for him to do it. Neither one of them will budge. In the end, it's Kinsella who stoops to lift it.

'There now,' he says.

Out in the yard, my father throws the rhubarb onto the back seat, gets in behind the wheel and starts the engine.

'Good luck to ye,' he says, 'I hope this girl will give no trouble.' He turns to me then. 'Try not to fall into the fire, you.'

I watch him reverse, turn into the lane, and drive away. I hear the wheels slam over the cattle grid, then the changing of gears and the noise of the motor going back the road we came. Why did he leave without so much as a good-bye, without ever mentioning that he would come back for me? The strange, ripe breeze that's crossing the yard feels cooler now, and big white clouds have marched in across the barn.

'What's ailing you, Child?' the woman says.

I look at my feet, dirty in my sandals.

Kinsella stands in close. 'Whatever it is, tell us. We won't mind.'

'Lord God Almighty, didn't he go and forget all about your bits and bobs!' the woman says. 'No wonder you're in a state. Well, hasn't he a head like a sieve, the same man.'

'Not a word about it,' Kinsella says. 'We'll have you togged out in no time.'

'There won't be a word about it this time twelve months,' the woman says.

They laugh hard for a moment then stop. When I follow the woman back inside, I want her to say something, to put my mind at ease. Instead, she clears the table, picks up the sharp knife and stands in the light under the window, washing the blade under the running tap. She stares at me as she wipes it clean, and puts it away.

'Now, Girleen,' she says. 'I think it's nearly time you had a bath.'

2

Beyond the kitchen, carpeted steps lead to an open room. There's a big double bed with a candlewick spread, and lamps at either side. This, I know, is where they sleep, and I'm glad, for some reason, that they sleep together. The woman takes me through to a bathroom, plugs a drain and turns the taps on full. The bath fills and the white room changes so that a type of blindness comes over us; we can see everything and yet we can't see.

'Hands up,' she says, and takes my dress off.

She tests the water and I step in, trusting her, but the water is too hot.

'Get in,' she says.

'It's too hot.'

'You'll get used to it.'

I put one foot through the steam and feel, again, the same, rough scald. I keep my foot in the water, and then, when I think I can't stand it any longer, my thinking changes, and I can. This water is deeper than any I have ever bathed in. Our mother bathes us in what little she can, and makes us share. After a while, I lie back and through the steam watch the woman as she scrubs my feet. The dirt under my nails she prises out with tweezers. She squeezes shampoo from a plastic bottle, lathers my hair and rinses the lather off. Then she makes me stand and soaps me all over with a cloth. Her hands are like my mother's hands but there is something else in them too, something I have never felt before and have no name for. I feel at such a loss for words but this is a new place, and new words are needed.

'Now your clothes,' she says.

'I don't have any clothes.'

'Of course you don't.' She pauses. 'Would some of our old things do you for now?'

'I don't mind.'

'Good girl.'

She takes me to another bedroom past theirs, at the other side of the stairs, and looks through a chest of drawers.

'Maybe these will fit you.'

She is holding a pair of old-fashioned trousers and a new plaid shirt. The sleeves and legs are too long but she rolls them up, and tightens the waist with a canvas belt, to fit me.

'There now,' she says.

'Mammy says I have to change my pants every day.'

'And what else does your mammy say?'

'She says you can keep me for as long as you like.'

She laughs at this and brushes the knots out of my hair, and turns quiet. The windows in this room are open and through these I see a stretch of lawn, a vegetable garden, edible things growing in rows, red spiky dahlias, a crow with something in his beak which he slowly breaks in two and eats, one half and then the other.

'Come down to the well with me,' she says.

'Now?'

'Does now not suit you?'

Something about the way she says this makes me wonder if it's something we are not supposed to do.

'Is this a secret?'

'What?'

'I mean, am I not supposed to tell?'

She turns me round, to face her. I have not really looked into her eyes, until now. Her eyes are dark blue pebbled with other blues. In this light she has a moustache.

'There are no secrets in this house, do you hear?'

I don't want to answer back but feel she wants an answer.

'Do you hear me?'

'Yeah.'

'It's not "yeah." It's "yes." What is it?'

13

'It's yes.'

'Yes, what?'

'Yes, there are no secrets in this house.'

'Where there's a secret,' she says, 'there's shame, and shame is something we can do without.'

'Okay.' I take big breaths so I won't cry.

She puts her arm around me. 'You're just too young to understand.'

As soon as she says this, I realise she is just like everyone else, and wish I was back at home so that all the things I do not understand could be the same as they always are.

Downstairs, she fetches the zinc bucket from the scullery and takes me down the fields. At first I feel uneasy in the strange clothes but walking along I forget. Kinsella's fields are broad and level, divided in strips with electric fences she says I must not touch, unless I want a shock. When the wind blows, sections of the longer grass bend over, turning silver. On one strip of land, tall Friesian cows stand all around us, grazing. Some of them look up as we pass but not one of them moves away. They have huge bags of milk and long teats. I can hear them pulling the grass up from the roots. The breeze, crossing the rim of the bucket, whispers as we walk along. Neither one of us talks, the way people sometimes don't when they are happy. As soon as I have this thought I realise its opposite is also true. We climb over a stile and follow a dry path worn through the grass. The path snakes through a long field over which white butterflies skim and dart, and we wind up at a small iron gate where stone steps run down to a well. The woman leaves the bucket on the grass and comes down with me.

'Look,' she says, 'what water is here. Who'd ever think there wasn't so much as a shower since the first of the month?'

I go down steps until I reach the water. I breathe and I hear the sound my breath makes over the still mouth of the well so I breathe harder for a while to feel these sounds I make, coming back. The woman stands behind, not seeming to mind each breath coming back, as though they were hers.

'Taste it,' she says.

'What?'

'Use the dipper.' She points.

Hanging over us is a big ladle, a shadow cupped in the dusty steel. I reach up and take it from the nail. She holds the belt of my trousers so I won't fall in.

'It's deep,' she says. 'Be careful.'

The sun, at a slant now, throws a rippled version of how we look back at us. For a moment, I am afraid. I wait until I see myself not as I was when I arrived, looking like a tinker's child, but as I am now, clean, in different clothes, with the woman behind me. I dip the ladle and bring it to my lips. This water is cool and clean as anything I have ever tasted: it tastes of my father leaving, of him never having been there, of having nothing after he was gone. I dip it again and lift it level with the sunlight. I drink six measures of water and wish, for now, that this place without shame or secrets could be my home. Then the woman pulls me back to where I am safe on the grass, and goes down alone. I hear the bucket floating on its side for a moment before it sinks and swallows, making a grateful sound, a glug, before it's torn away and lifted.

Walking back along the path and through the fields, holding her hand, I feel I have her balanced. Without me, I am certain she would tip over. I wonder how she manages when I am not here, and conclude that she must ordinarily fetch two buckets. I try to remember another time when I felt like this and am sad because I can't remember a time and happy, too, because I cannot.

That night, I expect her to make me kneel down but instead she tucks me in and tells me I can say a few little prayers in my bed, if that is what I ordinarily do. The light of the day is still shining bright and strong. She is just about to hang a blanket over the curtain rail, to block it out, when she pauses.

'Would you rather I left it?'

'Yeah.' I say. 'Yes.'

'Are you afraid of the dark?'

I want to say I am afraid but am too afraid to say so.

'Never mind,' she says. 'It doesn't matter. You can use the toilet past our room but there's a chamber pot there too, if you'd prefer.'

'I'll be alright,' I say.

'Is your mammy alright?'

'What do you mean?'

'Your mammy. Is she alright?'

'She used to get sick in the mornings but now she doesn't.'

'Why isn't the hay in?'

'She hasn't enough to pay the man. She only just paid him for last year.'

'God help her.' She smoothes the sheet across me, pleats it. 'Do you think she would be offended if I sent her a few bob?'

'Offended?'

'Do you think she'd mind?'

I think about this for a while, think about being my mother. 'She wouldn't but Da would.'

'Ah yes,' she says. 'Your father.'

She leans over me then and kisses me, a plain kiss, and says good-night. I sit up when she is gone and look around the room. Trains of every colour race across the wallpaper. There are no tracks for these trains but here and there a small boy stands off in the distance, waving. He looks happy but some part of me feels sorry for every version of him. I roll onto my side and, though I know she wants neither, wonder if my mother will have a girl or a boy this time. I think of my sisters who will not yet be in bed. They will have thrown their clay buns against the gable wall of the outhouse, and when the rain comes, the clay will soften and turn to mud. Everything changes into something else, turns into some version of what it was before.

I stay awake for as long as I can, then make myself get up and use the chamber pot, but only a dribble comes out. I go back to bed, more than half afraid, and fall asleep. At some point later in the night—it feels much later—the woman comes in. I grow still and breathe as though I have not wakened. I feel the mattress sinking, the weight of her on the bed.

'God help you, Child,' she says. 'If you were mine, I'd never leave you in a house with strangers.'

3

I wake in this new place to the old feeling of being hot and cold, all at once. Mrs Kinsella does not notice until later in the day, when she is stripping the bed.

'Lord God Almighty,' she says.

'What?'

'Would you look?' she says.

'What?'

I want to tell her, right now, to admit to it and be sent home so it will be over.

'These old mattresses,' she says, 'they weep. They're always weeping. What was I thinking of, putting you on this?'

We drag it down the stairs, out into the sunlit yard. The hound comes up and sniffs it, ready to cock his leg.

'Get off, you!' she shouts in an iron voice.

'What's all this?' Kinsella has come in from the fields.

'It's the mattress,' she says. 'The bloody thing is weeping. Didn't I say it was damp in that room?'

'In fairness,' he says, 'you did. But you shouldn't have dragged that down the stairs on your own.'

'I wasn't on my own,' she says. 'I had help.'

We scrub it with detergent and hot water and leave it there in the sun to dry.

'That's terrible,' she says. 'A terrible start, altogether. After all that, I think we need a rasher.'

She heats up the pan and fries rashers and tomatoes cut in halves with the cut side down. She likes to cut things up, to scrub and have things tidy, and to call things what they are. 'Rashers,' she says, putting the rashers on the spitting pan. 'Run out there and pull a few scallions, good girl.'

I run out to the vegetable garden, pull scallions and run back in, fast as I can, as though the house is on fire and it's water I've been sent for. I'm wondering if there's enough but the woman laughs.

'Well, we'll not run short, anyhow.'

She puts me in charge of the toast, lighting the grill for me, showing how the bread must be turned when one side is brown, as though this is something I haven't ever done but I don't really mind; she wants me to get things right, to teach me.

'Are we ready?'

'Yeah,' I say. 'Yes.'

'Good girl. Go out there and give himself a shout.'

I go out and call the call my mother taught me, up the fields.

Kinsella comes in a few minutes later, laughing. 'Now there's a shout and a half,' he says. 'I doubt there's a child in Wexford with a finer set of lungs.' He washes his hands and dries them, sits in at the table and butters his bread. The butter is soft, slipping off the knife, spreading easily.

'They said on the early news that another striker is dead.'

'Not another?'

'Aye. He passed during the night, poor man. Isn't it a terrible state of affairs?'

'God rest him,' the woman says. 'It's no way to die.'

'Wouldn't it make you grateful, though?' he says. 'A man starved himself to death and here I am on a fine day wud two women feeding me.'

'Haven't you earned it?' the woman says.

'I don't know have I,' he says. 'But it's happening anyway.'

All through the day, I help the woman around the house. She shows me the big, white machine that plugs in, a freezer where what she calls 'perishables' can be stored for months without rotting. We make ice cubes, go over every inch of the floors with a hoovering machine, dig new potatoes, make coleslaw and two loaves, and then she takes the clothes in off the line while they are still damp and sets up a board and starts ironing. She is like the man, doing it all without rushing but neither one of them ever really stops. Kinsella comes in and makes tea for all of us and drinks it standing up with a handful of Kimberley biscuits, then goes back out again.

Later, he comes in looking for me.

'Is the wee girl there?' he calls.

I run out to the door.

'Can you run?'

'What?'

'Are you fast on your feet?' he says.

'Sometimes,' I say.

'Well, run down there to the end of the lane as far as the box and run back.'

'The box?' I say.

'The post box. You'll see it there. Be as fast as you can.'

I take off, racing, to the end of the lane and find the box and get the letters and race back. Kinsella is looking at his watch.

'Not bad,' he says, 'for your first time.'

He takes the letters from me. There's four in all, nothing in my mother's hand.

'Do you think there's money in any of these?'

'I don't know.'

'Ah, you'd know if there was, surely. The women can smell money. Do you think there's news?'

'I wouldn't know,' I say.

'Do you think there's a wedding invitation?'

I want to laugh.

'It wouldn't be yours anyhow,' he says. 'You're too young to be getting married. Do you think you'll get married?'

'I don't know,' I say. 'Mammy says I shouldn't take a present of a man.'

Kinsella laughs. 'She could be right there. Still and all, there's no two men the same. And it'd be a swift man that would catch you, Long Legs. We'll try you again tomorrow and see if we can't improve your time.'

'I've to go faster?'

'Oh aye,' he says. 'By the time you're ready for home you'll be like a reindeer. There'll not be a man in the parish will catch you without a long-handled net and a racing bike.'

That night, after supper, when Kinsella is reading his newspaper in the parlour, the woman sits down at the cooker and tells me she is working on her complexion.

'It's a secret,' she says. 'Not many people know about this.'

She takes a packet of Weetabix out of the cupboard and eats one of them not with milk in a bowl but dry, out of her hand. 'Look at me,' she says. 'I haven't so much as a pimple.'

And sure enough, she doesn't. Her skin is clear.

'But you said there were no secrets here.'

'This is different, more like a secret recipe.'

She hands me one, then another and watches as I eat them. They taste a bit like the dry bark of a tree must taste but I don't really care, as some part of me is pleased to please her. I eat five in all during the nine o'clock news while they show the mother of the dead striker, a riot, then the Taoiseach and then foreign people out in Africa, starving to death and then the weather forecast, which says the days are to be fine for another week or so. The woman sits me on her lap through it all and idly strokes my bare feet.

'You have nice long toes,' she says. 'Nice feet.'

Later, she makes me lie down on the bed before I go to sleep and cleans the wax out of my ears with a hair clip.

'You could have planted a geranium in what was there,' she says. 'Does your mammy not clean out your ears?'

'She hasn't always time,' I say, guarded.

'I suppose the poor woman doesn't,' she says. 'What with all of ye.'

She takes the hairbrush then and I can hear her counting under her breath to a hundred and then she stops and plaits it loosely. I fall asleep fast that night and when I wake, the old feeling is not there.

Later that afternoon, when Mrs Kinsella is making the bed, she looks at me, pleased.

'Your complexion is better already, see?' she says. 'All you need is minding.'

4

And so the days pass. I keep waiting for something to happen, for the ease I feel to end—to wake in a wet bed, to make some blunder, some big gaffe, to break something— but each day follows on much like the one before. We wake early with the sun coming in and have eggs of one kind or another with porridge and toast for breakfast. Kinsella puts on his cap and goes back out to the yard. Myself and the woman make a list out loud of jobs that need to be done, and just do them: we pull rhubarb, make tarts, paint the skirting boards, take all the bedclothes out of the hot press and hoover out the spider webs and put all the clean clothes back in again, make scones, scrub the bathtub, sweep the staircase, polish the furniture, boil onions for onion sauce and put it in containers in the freezer, pull the weeds out of the flower beds and then, when the sun goes down, water things. Then it's a matter of supper and the walk across the fields and to the well. Every evening the television is turned on for the nine o'clock news and then, after the forecast, I'm told it is time for bed.

Sometimes people come into the house at night. I can hear them playing cards and talking. They curse and accuse each other of reneging and dealing off the bottom, and coins are thrown into what sounds like a tin dish, and sometimes all the coins are emptied out into what sounds like a stash that's already there. Once somebody came in and played the spoons. Once there was something that sounded just like a donkey, and the woman came up to fetch me, saying I may as well come down, as nobody could get a wink of sleep with the Ass Casey in the house. I went down and ate macaroons and then two men came to the door selling lines for a raffle whose proceeds, they said, would go towards putting a new roof on the school.

'Of course,' Kinsella said.

'We didn't really think—'

'Come on in,' Kinsella said. 'Just cos I've none of my own doesn't mean I'd see the rain falling in on anyone else's.'

And so they came in and more tea was made and the woman emptied out the ashtray and dealt the cards and said she hoped the present generation of children in that school, if they were inclined towards cards, would learn the rules of forty-five properly because it was clear that this particular generation was having difficulties, that some people weren't at all clear on how to play, except for sometimes, when it suited them.

'Oh, there's shots!'

'You have to listen to thunder.'

'Aisy knowing whose purse is running low.'

'It's ahead, I am,' she said. 'And it's ahead I'll be when it's over.'

And this, for some reason, made the Ass Casey bray, which made me laugh and then they all started laughing until one of the men said, 'Is it a tittering match we have here or are we going to play cards?' which made the Ass Casey bray once more, and it started all over again.

5

One afternoon, while we are topping and tailing gooseberries for jam, when the job is more than half done and the sugar is already weighed and the pots warmed, Kinsella comes in from the yard and washes and dries his hands and looks at me in a way he has never done before.

'I think it's past time we got you togged out, Girl.'

I am wearing a pair of navy blue trousers and a blue shirt the woman took from the chest of drawers.

'What's wrong with her?' the woman says.

'Tomorrow's Sunday, and she needs something more than that for Mass,' he says. 'I'll not have her going as she went last week.'

'Sure isn't she clean and tidy?'

'You know what I'm talking about, Edna.' He sighs. 'Why don't you go up there and change and I'll run us all into Gorey.'

The woman keeps on picking the gooseberries from the

colander, stretching her hand out, but a little more slowly each time, for the next one. At one point I think she will stop but she keeps on until she is finished and then she gets up and places the colander on the sink and lets out a sound I've never heard anyone make, and slowly goes upstairs.

Kinsella looks at me and smiles a hard kind of a smile then looks over to the window ledge where a sparrow has come down to perch and readjust her wings. The little bird seems uneasy—as though she can scent the cat, who sometimes sits there. Kinsella's eyes are not quite still in his head. It's as though there's a big piece of trouble stretching itself out in the back of his mind. He toes the leg of a chair and looks over at me.

'You should wash your hands and face before you go to town,' he says. 'Didn't your father even bother to teach you that much?'

I freeze in the chair, waiting for something much worse to happen, but Kinsella does nothing more; he just stands there, locked in the wash of his own speech. As soon as he turns, I race for the stairs but when I reach the bathroom, the door won't open.

'It's alright,' the woman says, after a while from inside and then, shortly afterwards, opens it. 'Sorry for keeping you.' She has been crying but she isn't ashamed. 'It'll be nice for you to have some clothes of your own,' she says then, wiping her eyes. 'And Gorey is a nice town. I don't know why I didn't think of taking you there before now.'

Town is a crowded place with a wide main street. Outside

the shops, so many different things are hanging in the sun. There are plastic nets full of beach balls, blow-up toys. A see-through dolphin looks as though he is shivering in a cold breeze. There are plastic spades and matching buckets, moulds for sand castles, grown men digging ice cream out of tubs with little plastic spoons, potted plants that feel hairy to the touch, a man in a van selling dead fish.

Kinsella reaches into his pocket and hands me something. 'You'll get a Choc-ice out of that.'

I open my hand and stare at the pound note.

'Couldn't she buy half a dozen Choc-ices out of that,' the woman says.

'Ah, what is she for, only for spoiling?' Kinsella says.

'What do you say?' the woman says.

'Thanks,' I say. 'Thank you.'

'Well, stretch it out and spend it well,' Kinsella laughs.

The woman takes me to the draper's where she buys a packet of darning needles at a counter and four yards of oilcloth printed with yellow pears. Then we go upstairs where the clothing is kept. She picks out cotton dresses and some pants and trousers and a few tops and we go in behind a curtain so I can try them on.

'Isn't she tall?' says the assistant.

'We're all tall,' says the woman.

'She's the spit and image of her mammy. I can see it now,' the assistant says, and then says the lilac dress is the best fit and the most flattering, and the woman agrees. She buys me a printed blouse, too, with short sleeves much like the one she wore the day I came, dark blue trousers, and a pair of black leather shoes with a little strap and a buckle on the front, some panties and white ankle socks. The girl hands her the docket, and she takes out her purse and pays for it all.

'Well may you wear,' the assistant says. 'Isn't your mammy good to you?'

Out in the street, the sun feels strong again, blinding. Some part of me wishes it would go away, that it would cloud over so I could see properly. We meet people the woman knows. Some of these people stare at me and ask who I am. One of them has a new baby in a pushchair. Mrs Kinsella bends down and coos and he slobbers a little and starts to cry.

'He's making strange,' the mother says. 'Pay no heed.'

We meet another woman with eyes like picks, who asks whose child I am, who I am belonging to? When she is told, she says, 'Ah, isn't she company for you all the same, God help you.'

Mrs Kinsella stiffens. 'You must excuse me,' she says, 'but this man of mine is waiting and you know what these men are like.'

'Like fecking bulls, they are,' the woman says. 'Haven't an ounce of patience.'

'God forgive me but if I ever run into that woman again it will be too soon,' says Mrs Kinsella, when we have turned the corner.

We go to the butchers for rashers and sausages and a horseshoe of black pudding, to the chemist where she asks for Aunt Acid, and then on down to a little shop she calls the gift gallery where they sell cards and notepaper and pretty pieces of jewellery from a case of revolving shelves.

'Isn't your mammy's birthday coming up shortly?'

'Yes,' I say, without being sure.

'We'll get a card for her, so.'

She tells me to choose, and I pick a card with a frightened looking cat sitting in front of a bed of yellow flowers.

'Not long now till they'll be back to school,' says the woman behind the counter. 'Isn't it a great relief to have them off your back?'

'This one is no trouble,' Mrs Kinsella says, and pays for the card along with some sheets of notepaper and a packet of envelopes. 'It's only missing her I'll be when she is gone.'

'Humph,' the woman says.

Before we go back to the car she lets me loose in a sweet shop. I take my time choosing, hand over the pound note and take back the change.

'Didn't you stretch it well,' she says, when I come out.

Kinsella is parked in the shade, with the windows open, reading the newspaper.

'Well?' he says. 'Did ye get sorted?'

'Aye,' she says.

'Grand,' he says.

I give him the Choc-ice and her the Flake and lie on the back seat eating the hard gums, careful not to choke as we cross over bumps in the road. I listen to the change rattling in my pocket, the wind rushing through the car and their talk, scraps of news being shared between them in the front.

When we turn into the yard, another car is parked outside the door. A woman is on the front step, pacing, with her arms crossed.

'Isn't that Harry Redmond's girl?'

'I don't like the look of this,' says Kinsella.

'Oh, John,' she says, rushing over. 'I'm sorry to trouble you but didn't our Michael pass away and there's not a soul at home. They're all out on the combines and won't be back till God knows what hour and I've no way of getting word to them. We're rightly stuck. Would you ever come down and give us a hand digging the grave?'

'I don't know that this'll be any place for you but I can't leave you here,' the woman says, later that same day. 'So get ready and we'll go, in the name of God.'

I go upstairs and change into the new dress, the ankle socks and shoes.

'Don't you look nice,' she says, when I come down. 'John's not always easy but he's hardly ever wrong.'

Walking down the road, there's a taste of something darker in the air, of something that might come and fall and change things. We pass houses whose doors and windows are wide open, long, flapping clotheslines, gravelled entrances to other lanes. At the bend, a bay pony is leaning up against a gate, but when I reach out to stroke his nose, he whinnies and canters off. Outside a cottage, a black dog with curls all down his back comes out and barks at us, hotly, through the bars of a gate. At the first crossroads, we meet a heifer who panics and finally races past us, lost. All through the walk, the wind blows hard and soft and hard again through the tall, flowering hedges, the high trees. In the fields, the combines are out cutting the wheat, the barley and oats, saving the corn, leaving behind long rows of straw. We meet men on tractors, going in different directions, pulling balers to the fields, and trailers full of grain to the co-op. Birds swoop down, brazen, eating the fallen seed off the middle of the road. Further along, we meet two barechested men, their eyes so white in faces so tanned and dusty.

The woman stops to greet them and tells them where we are going.

'God rest him. Didn't he go quick in the end?' one man says.

'Aye,' says the other. 'But didn't he reach his three score and ten? What more can any of us hope for?'

We keep on walking, standing in tight to the hedges, the ditches, letting things pass.

'Have you been to a wake before?' the woman asks.

'I don't think so.'

'Well, I might as well tell you: there will be a dead man here in a coffin and lots of people and some of them might have a little too much taken.'

'What will they be taking?'

'Drink,' she says.

When we come to the house, several men are leaning against a low wall, smoking. There's a black ribbon on the door and hardly a light shining from the house but when we go in, the kitchen is bright, and packed with people who are talking. The woman who asked Kinsella to dig the grave is

CLAIRE KEEGAN

there, making sandwiches. There are big bottles of red and white lemonade, stout, and in the middle of all this, a big wooden box with an old dead man lying inside of it. His hands are joined as though he had died praying, a string of rosary beads around his fingers. Some of the men are sitting around the coffin, using the part that's closed as a counter on which to rest their glasses. One of these is Kinsella.

'There she is,' he says. 'Long Legs. Come over here.'

He pulls me onto his lap, and gives me a sip from his glass.

'Do you like the taste of that?'

'No.'

He laughs. 'Good girl. Don't ever get a taste for it. If you start, you might never stop and then you'd wind up like the rest of us.'

He pours red lemonade into a cup for me. I sit on his lap drinking it and eating the queen cakes out of the biscuit tin and looking at the dead man, hoping his eyes will open.

The people come and go, drifting in and out, shaking hands, drinking and eating and looking at the dead man, saying what a lovely corpse he is, and doesn't he look happy now that his end has come, and who was it that laid him out? They talk of the forecast and the moisture content of corn, of milk quotas and the next general election. I feel myself getting heavy on Kinsella's lap.

'Am I getting heavy?'

'Heavy?' he says. 'You're like a feather, Child. Stay where you are.'

I put my head against him but I'm bored and wish there

32

were things to do, other children who would play.

'The girl's getting uneasy,' I hear the woman say.

'What's ailing her?' says another.

'Ah, it's no place for the child, really,' she says. 'It's just I didn't like not to come, and I wouldn't leave her behind.'

'Sure I'll take her home with me, Edna. I'm going now. Can't you call in and collect her on your way?'

'Oh,' she says. 'I don't know should I.'

'Mine'd be a bit of company for her. Can't they play away out the back? And that man there won't budge as long as he has her on his knee.'

Mrs Kinsella laughs. I've never heard her laugh like this.

'Sure maybe, if you don't mind, you would, Mildred,' she says. 'What harm is in it? And you know we'll not be long after you.'

'Not a bother,' the woman says.

When we are out on the road, and the good-byes are said, Mildred strides on into a pace I can just about keep, and as soon as she rounds the bend, the questions start. She is eaten alive with curiosity; hardly is one question answered before the next is fired: 'Which room did they put you into? Did Kinsella give you money? How much? Does she drink at night? Does he? Are they playing cards up there much? Who was there? What were they selling the lines for? Do ye say the rosary? Does she put butter or margarine in her pastry? Where does the old dog sleep? Is the freezer packed solid? Does she skimp on things or is she allowed to spend? Are the child's clothes still hanging in the wardrobe?'

I answer them all easily, until the last.

'The child's clothes?'

'Aye,' she says. 'Sure if you're sleeping in his room you must surely know. Did you not look?'

'Well, she had clothes I wore for all the time I was here but we went to Gorey this morning and bought all new things.'

'This rig-out you're wearing now? God Almighty,' she says. 'Anybody would think you were going on for a hundred.'

'I like it,' I say. 'They told me it was flattering.'

'Flattering, is it? Well. Well,' she says. 'I suppose it is, after living in the dead's clothes all this time.'

'What?'

'The Kinsella's young lad, you dope. Did you not know?'

I don't know what to say.

'That must have been some stone they rolled back to find you. Sure didn't he follow that auld hound of theirs into the slurry tank and drown? That's what they say happened anyhow,' she says.

I keep on walking and try not to think about what she has said even though I can think of little else. The time for the sun to go down is getting close but the day feels like it isn't ending. I look at the sky and see the sun, still high, and clouds, and, far away, a round moon coming out.

'They say John got the gun and took the hound down the field but he hadn't the heart to shoot him, the softhearted fool.'

We walk on between the bristling hedges in which small things seem to rustle and move. Chamomile grows along these ditches, wood sage and mint, plants whose names my mother somehow found the time to teach me. Further along, the same lost heifer is still lost, in a different part of the road.

'And you know, the pair of them turned white overnight.'

'What do you mean?'

'Their hair, what else?'

'But Mrs Kinsella's hair is black.'

'Black? Aye, black out of the dye-pot, you mean.' She laughs.

I wonder at her laughing like this. I wonder at the clothes and how I'd worn them and the boy in the wallpaper and how I never put it all together. Soon we come to the place where the black dog is barking through the bars of the gate.

'Shut up and get in, you,' she says to him.

It's a cottage she lives in with uneven slabs of concrete outside the front door, overgrown shrubs, and tall Red Hot Pokers growing out of the ground. Here I must watch my head, my step. When we go in, the place is cluttered and an older woman is smoking at the cooker. There's a baby in a high chair. He lets out a cry when he sees the woman and drops a handful of marrowfat peas over the edge.

'Look at you,' she says. 'The state of you.'

I'm not sure if it's the woman or the child she is talking to. She takes off her cardigan and sits down and starts talking about the wake: who was there, the type of sandwiches that were made, the queen cakes, the corpse who was lying up crooked in the coffin and hadn't even been shaved properly, how they had plastic rosary beads for him, the poor fucker.

I don't know whether to sit or stand, to listen or leave but just as I'm deciding what to do, the dog barks and the gate opens and Kinsella comes in, stooping under the door frame.

'Good evening all,' he says.

'Ah, John,' the woman says. 'You weren't long. We're only in the door. Aren't we only in the door, Child?'

'Yes.'

Kinsella hasn't taken his eyes off me. 'Thanks, Mildred. It was good of you, to take her home.'

'It was nothing,' the woman says. 'She's a quiet young one, this.'

'She says what she has to say, and no more. May there be many like her,' he says. 'Are you ready to come home, Petal?'

I get up and he says a few more things, to smooth things over, the way people do. I follow him out to the car where the woman is waiting.

'Were you alright in there?' she says.

I say I was.

'Did she ask you anything?'

'A few things, nothing much.'

'What did she ask you?'

'She asked me if you used butter of margarine in your pastry.'

'Did she ask you anything else?'

'She asked me was the freezer packed tight.'

'There you are,' says Kinsella.

'Did she tell you anything?' the woman asks.

I don't know what to say.

'What did she tell you?'

'She told me you had a little boy who followed the dog into the slurry tank and died, and that I wore his clothes to Mass last Sunday.'

When we get home, the hound gets up and comes out to the car to greet us. It's only now I realise I've not heard either one of them call him by his name. Kinsella sighs and goes off to milk. When he comes inside, he says he's not ready for bed and that there will be no visitors tonight anyhow, on account of the wake—not, he says, that he wants any. The woman goes upstairs and changes and comes back down in her nightdress. Kinsella has taken my shoes off and has put what I now know is the boy's jacket on me.

'What are you doing now?' she says.

'What does it look like? And she'll break her neck in these.'

He goes out, stumbling a little, then comes back in with a sheet of sandpaper and scuffs up the soles of my new shoes so I will not slip.

'Come on,' he says. 'We'll break them in.'

'Didn't she already break them in? Where are you taking her?'

'Only as far as the strand,' he says.

'You'll be careful with that girl, John Kinsella,' she says. 'And don't you go without the lamp.'

'What need is there for a lamp on a night like tonight?' he says, but he takes it anyhow, as it's handed to him.

There's a big moon shining on the yard, chalking our way

onto the lane and along the road. Kinsella takes my hand in his. As soon as he takes it, I realise my father has never once held my hand, and some part of me wants Kinsella to let me go so I won't have to feel this. It's a hard feeling but as we walk along I begin to settle and let the difference between my life at home and the one I have here be. He takes small steps so we can walk in time. I think about the woman in the cottage, of how she walked and spoke, and conclude that there are huge differences between people.

When we reach the crossroads we turn right, down a steep, sloping road. The wind is high and hoarse in the trees, tearing fretfully through the dry boughs, and their leaves rise and swing. It's sweet to feel the open road falling away under us, knowing we will, at its end, come to the sea. The road goes on and the sky, everything, seems to get brighter. Kinsella says a few meaningless things along the way then falls into the quiet way he has about him, and time passes without seeming to pass and then we are in a sandy, open space where people must park cars. It is full of tyre marks and potholes, a rubbish bin which seems not to have been emptied in a long time.

'We're almost there now, Petal.'

He leads me up a steep hill where, on either side, tall rushes bend and shake. My feet sink in the deep sand, and the climb takes my breath away. Then we are standing on the crest of a dark place where the land ends and there is a long strand and water which I know is deep and stretches all the way to England. Far out, in the darkness, two bright lights are blinking.

Kinsella lets me loose and I race down the far side of the dune to the place where the black sea hisses up into loud, frothy waves. I run towards them as they back away and run back, shrieking, when another crashes in. When Kinsella catches up, we take our shoes off. In places we walk along with the edge of the sea clawing at the sand under our bare feet. In places he leaves me to run. At one point we go in until the water is up to his knees and he holds me on his shoulders.

'Don't be afraid!' he says.

'What?'

'Don't be afraid!'

The strand is all washed clean, without so much as a footprint. There's a crooked line, close to the dunes, where things have washed up: plastic bottles, sticks, the handle of a mop whose head is lost and, further on, a stable door, its bolt broken.

'Some man's horse is loose tonight,' Kinsella says. He walks on for a while then. It is quieter up here, away from the noise of the sea. 'You know the fishermen sometimes find horses out at sea. A man I know towed a colt in one time and the horse lay down for a long time before he got up. And he was perfect. Tiredness was all it was, after being out so long.

'Strange things happen,' he says. 'A strange thing happened to you tonight but Edna meant no harm. It's too good, she is. She wants to find the good in others, and sometimes her way of finding that is to trust them, hoping she'll not be disappointed but she sometimes is.'

He laughs then, a queer, sad laugh. I don't know what to say.

'You don't ever have to say anything,' he says. 'Always remember that as a thing you need never do. Many's the man lost much just because he missed a perfect opportunity to say nothing.'

Everything about the night feels strange: to walk to a sea that's always been there, to see it and feel it and fear it in the half dark, and to listen to this man saying things about horses out at sea, about his wife trusting others so she'll learn who not to trust, things I don't fully understand, things which may not even be intended for me.

We keep on walking until we come to a place where the cliffs and rocks come out to meet the water. Now that we can go no farther, we must turn back. Maybe the way back will somehow make sense of the coming. Here and there, flat white shells lie shining and washed up on the sand. I stoop to gather them. They feel smooth and clean and brittle in my hands. We turn back along the beach and walk on, seeming to walk a greater distance than the one we crossed in reaching the place where we could not pass, and then the moon disappears behind a darkish cloud and we cannot see where we are going. At this point, Kinsella lets out a sigh, stops, and lights the lamp.

'Ah, the women are nearly always right, all the same,' he says. 'Do you know what the women have a gift for?'

'What?'

'Eventualities. A good woman can look far down the line and smell what's coming before a man even gets a sniff of it.'

He shines the light along the strand to find our footprints, to follow them back, but the only prints he can find are mine.

'You must have carried me there,' he says.

I laugh at the thought of me carrying him, at the impossibility, then realise it was a joke, and that I got it.

When the moon comes out again, he turns the lamp off and by the moon's light we easily find and follow the path we took out of the dunes. When we reach the top, he won't let me put my shoes on but does it for me. Then he does his own and knots the laces. We stand then, to pause and look back out at the water.

'See, there's three lights now where there was only two before.'

I look out across the sea. There, the two lights are blinking as before, but with another, steady light, shining in between.

'Can you see it?' he says.

'I can,' I say. 'It's there.'

And that is when he puts his arms around me and gathers me into them as though I were his.

6

After a week of rain, on a Thursday, the letter comes. It is not so much a surprise as a shock. Already I have seen the signs: the shampoo for head lice in the chemist's shop, the fine tooth combs. In the gift gallery there are copy books stacked high and different coloured biros, rulers, mechanical drawing sets. In the hardware, the lunchboxes and satchels and hurling sticks are left out front, where the women can see them.

We come home and take soup, dipping our bread, breaking it, slurping a little, now that we know each other. Afterwards, I follow Kinsella out to the hayshed where he makes me promise not to look while he is welding. I am following him around today, I realise, but I cannot help it. It is past the time for the post to come but he does not suggest I fetch it until evening, until the cows are milked and the milking parlour is swept and scrubbed.

'I think it's time,' he says, washing his boots with the hose.

I get into position, using the front step as a starting block. Kinsella looks at the watch and slices the air with his hand. I take off, race down the yard, the lane, make a tight corner, open the box, get the letters, and race back to the step, knowing my time was not as fast as yesterday's.

'Nineteen seconds faster than your first run,' Kinsella says. 'And a two second improvement on yesterday, despite the heavy ground. It's like the wind, you are.'

He takes the letters and goes through them, but today, instead of making jokes about what's inside of each, he pauses.

'Is that from Mammy?'

'You know,' he says. 'I think it could be.'

'Do I have to go home?'

'Well, it's addressed to Edna so why don't we give it in to her and let her read it.'

We go into the parlour where she is sitting with her feet up, looking through a book of knitting patterns. There's a coal fire in the grate, and little plumes of black smoke sliding back down into the room.

'This chimney, we never got it cleaned, John. I'm sure there must be a crow's nest in it.'

Kinsella slides the letter onto her lap, over what she is reading. She sits up, opens the letter and reads it. It's one small sheet with writing on both sides. She puts it down then picks it up and reads it again.

'Well,' she says, 'you have a new brother. Nine pounds, two ounces.'

'Great,' I say.

'Don't be like that,' Kinsella says.

'What?' I say.

'And school starts on Monday,' she says. 'Your mother has asked us to leave you up at the weekend so she can get you togged out and all.'

'I have to go back then?'

'Aye,' she says. 'But sure didn't you know that?'

I nod and look at the letter.

'You couldn't stay here forever with us two old forgeries.'

I stand there and stare at the fire, trying not to cry. It is a long time since I have done this and, in doing it, remember that it is the worst thing you can possibly do. I don't so much hear as feel Kinsella leaving the room.

'Don't upset yourself,' the woman says. 'Come over here.'

She shows me pages with knitted jumpers and asks me which pattern I like best, but all the patterns seem to blur together and I just point to one, a blue one, which looks like it might be easy.

'Well, you would pick the hardest one in the book,' she says. 'I'd better get started on that this week or you'll be too big for it by the time it's knitted.

7

Now that I know I must go home, I almost want to go, to get it over with. I wake earlier than usual and look out at the wet fields, the dripping trees, the hills, which seem greener than they did when I came. I think back to this time and it seems so long ago, when I used to wet the bed and worry about breaking things. Kinsella hangs around all day doing things but not really finishing anything. He says he has no discs for his angle grinder, no welding rods, and he cannot find the vice grip. He says he got so many jobs done in the long stretch of fine weather that there's little left to do.

We are out looking at the calves, who are feeding. With warm water, Kinsella has made up their milk replacement which they suck from long, rubber teats until the teats run dry. It's an odd system, taking the calves off the cows and giving them milk replacement so Kinsella can milk their mothers and sell the milk, but they look content.

'Could ye leave me back this evening?'

'This evening?' Kinsella says.

I nod.

'Any evening suits me,' he says. 'I'll take you whenever you want, Petal.'

I look at the day. The day is like any other, with a flat grey sky hanging over the yard and the wet hound on watch outside the front door.

'Well, I had better milk early, so,' he says. 'Right,' and goes on down the yard past me as though I have already gone.

The woman gives me a brown leather bag. 'You can keep this old thing,' she says. 'I never have use for it.'

We fold my clothes and place them inside, along with the books we bought at Webb's in Gorey: *Heidi*, *What Katy Did Next*, *The Snow Queen*. At first, I struggled with some of the bigger words but Kinsella kept his fingernail under each, patiently, until I guessed it and then I did this by myself until I no longer needed to guess, and read on. It was like learning to ride the bike; I felt myself taking off, the freedom of going places I couldn't have gone before, and it was easy.

Mrs Kinsella gives me a bar of yellow soap and my facecloth, the hairbrush. As we gather all these things together, I remember the days we spent, where we got them, what was sometimes said, and how the sun, for most of the time, was shining.

Just then a car pulls into the yard. It's a neighbouring man I remember from the night of cards.

'Edna,' he says, in a panic. 'Is John about?'

'He's out at the milking,' she says. 'He should be finishing up now.'

He runs down the yard, heavy in his Wellington boots, and a minute later, Kinsella sticks his head around the door.

'Joe Fortune needs a hand pulling a calf,' he says. 'Would you ever just finish the parlour off? I have the herd out.'

'I will, surely,' she says.

'I'll be back just as soon as I can.'

'Don't I know you will.'

She puts on her anorak and goes down the yard to the milking parlour. I sit restless and wonder should I go out to help but come to the conclusion that I'd only be in the way. So I sit in the armchair and look out to where a watery light is trembling across the scullery, shining off the zinc bucket. I could go down to the well for water so she would have the well water for her tea when she gets back home tonight. It could be the last thing I do.

I put on the boy's jacket and take up the bucket and walk down the fields. I know the way along the track and past the cows, the electric fences, could find the well with my eyes closed. When I cross the stile the path does not look like the same path we followed on that first evening here. The way is muddy now and slippery in places. I trudge along, towards the little iron gate and down the steps. The water is much higher these days. I was on the fifth step that first evening here, but now I stand on the first and see the edge of the water reaching up and just about sucking the edge of the step that's one down from me. I stand there breathing, making the sounds for a while to hear them coming back, one last time. Then I bend down with the bucket, letting it float then swallow and sink as the woman does but when I reach out with my other hand to lift it, another hand just like mine seems to come out of the water and pull me in.

8

It is not that evening or the following one but the evening after, on the Sunday, that I am taken home. After I came back from the well, soaked to the skin, the woman took one look at me and turned very still before she gathered me up and took me inside and made up my bed again. The following morning, I didn't feel hot, but she kept me upstairs, bringing me hot drinks with lemon and cloves and honey, aspirin.

'Tis nothing but a chill, she has,' I heard Kinsella say.

'When I think of what could have happened.'

'If you've said that once, you've said it a hundred times.'

'But—'

'Nothing happened, and the girl is grand. And that's the end of it.'

I lie there with the hot-water bottle, listening to the rain and reading my books, following what happens more closely and making up something different to happen at the end of each, each time. I doze and have strange dreams: of the lost heifer panicking on the night strand, of bony, brown cows having no milk in their teats, of my mother climbing up and getting stuck in an apple tree. Then I wake and drink the broth and whatever else the woman gives me.

On Sunday, I am allowed to get up, and we pack everything again, as before. Towards evening, we have supper, and wash and change into our good clothes. The sun has come out, is lingering in long, cool slants, and the yard is dry in places. Sooner than I would like, we are ready and in the car, turning down the lane, going up through the street of Gorey and on back along the narrow roads through Carnew and Shillelagh.

'That's where Da lost the red heifer playing cards,' I say.

'Is that a fact?' Kinsella says.

'Wasn't that some wager?' says the woman.

'It was some loss for him,' says Kinsella.

We carry on through Parkbridge, over the hill where the old school stands, and on down towards our car-road. The gates in the lane are closed and Kinsella gets out to open them. He drives through, closes the gates behind him, and drives on very slowly to the house. I feel, now, that the woman is making up her mind as to whether or not she should say something but I don't really know what it is, and she gives me no clue. The car stops in front of the house, the dogs bark, and my sisters race out. I see my mother looking out through the window, with what is now the second youngest in her arms.

Inside, the house feels damp and cold. The lino is all tracked over with dirty footprints. Mammy stands there with my little brother, and looks at me.

'You've grown,' she says.

'Yes,' I say.

'"Yes," is it?' she says, and raises her eyebrows.

She bids the Kinsellas good evening and tells them to sit down—if they can find a place to sit—and fills the kettle from the bucket under the kitchen table. We take playthings off the car seat under the window, and sit down. Mugs are taken off the dresser, a loaf of bread is sliced, butter and jam left out.

'Oh, I brought you jam,' the woman says. 'Don't let me forget to give it to you, Mary.'

'I made this out of the rhubarb you sent down,' Ma says. 'That's the last of it.'

'I should have brought more,' the woman says. 'I wasn't thinking.'

'Where's the new addition?' Kinsella asks.

'Oh, he's up in the room there. You'll hear him soon enough.'

'Is he sleeping through the night for you?'

'On and off,' Ma says. 'The same child could crow at any hour.'

My sisters look at me as though I'm an English cousin, coming over to touch my dress, the buckles on my shoes. They seem different, thinner, and have nothing to say. We sit in to the table and eat the bread and drink the tea. When a cry is heard from upstairs, Ma gives my brother to Mrs Kinsella, and goes up to fetch the baby. The baby is pink and crying, his fists tight. He looks bigger than the last, stronger.

'Isn't there a fine child, God bless him,' Kinsella says.

'Isn't he a dote,' Mrs Kinsella says, holding on to the other.

Ma pours more tea for them all with one hand and sits down and takes her breast out for the baby. Her doing this in front of Kinsella makes me blush. Seeing me blush, Ma gives me a long, deep look.

'No sign of himself?' Kinsella says.

'He went out there earlier, wherever he's gone,' Ma says.

A little bit of talk starts up then, rolls back and forth, bumping between them for a while. Soon after, a car is heard outside. Nothing more is said until my father appears, and throws his hat on the dresser.

'Evening all,' he says.

'Dan,' says Kinsella.

'Ah there's the prodigal child,' he says. 'You came back to us, did you?'

I say I did.

'Did she give trouble?'

'Trouble?' Kinsella says. 'Good as gold, she was, the same girl.'

'Is that so?' says Da, sitting down. 'Well, isn't that a relief.'

'You'll want to sit in,' Mrs Kinsella says, 'and get your supper.'

'I had a liquid supper,' Da says, 'down in Parkbridge.'

Ma turns the baby to the other breast, and changes the subject. 'Have ye no news at all from down your way?'

'Not a stem,' says Kinsella. 'It's all quiet down with us.'

I sneeze then, and reach into my pocket for my handkerchief, and blow my nose.

'Have you caught cold?' Ma asks.

'No,' I say, hoarsely.

'You haven't?'

'Nothing happened.'

'What do you mean?'

'I didn't catch cold,' I say.

'I see,' she says, giving me another deep look.

'The child's been in the bed for the last couple of days,' says Kinsella. 'Didn't she catch herself a wee chill.'

'Aye,' says Da. 'You couldn't mind them. You know yourself.'

'Dan,' Ma says, in a steel voice.

Mrs Kinsella looks uneasy, like she was the day of the gooseberries.

'You know, I think it's nearly time that we were making tracks,' Kinsella says. 'It's a long road home.'

'Ah, what's the big hurry?' Ma says.

'No hurry at all, Mary, just the usual. These cows don't give you any opportunity to have a lie-in.'

He gets up then and takes my little brother from his wife and gives him to my father. My father takes the child and looks across at the baby suckling. I sneeze and blow my nose again.

'That's a right dose you came home with,' Da says.

'It's nothing she hasn't caught before and won't catch again,' Ma says. 'Sure isn't it going around?'

'Are you ready for home?' Kinsella asks.

Mrs Kinsella stands then and they say their good-byes and go outside. I follow them out to the car with my mother who still has the baby in her arms. Kinsella lifts out the box of jam, the four stone sack of potatoes.

'These are floury,' he says. 'Queens they are, Mary.'

We stand for a little while and then my mother thanks them, saying it was a lovely thing they did, to keep me.

'No bother at all,' says Kinsella.

'The girl was welcome and is welcome again, any time,' the woman says.

'She's a credit to you, Mary,' Kinsella says. 'You keep your head in the books,' he says to me. 'I want to see gold stars on them copy books next time I come up here.' He gives me a kiss then and the woman hugs me and then I watch them getting into the car and feel the doors closing and a start when the engine turns and the car begins to move away. Kinsella seems more eager to leave than he was in coming here.

'What happened at all?' Ma says, now that the car is gone.

'Nothing,' I say.

'Tell me.'

'Nothing happened.' This is my mother I am speaking to but I have learned enough, grown enough, to know that what happened is not something I need ever mention. It is my perfect opportunity to say nothing.

I hear the car braking on the gravel in the lane, the door opening, and then I am doing what I do best. It's nothing I have to think about. I take off from standing and race on down the lane. My heart does not so much feel that it is in my chest as in my hands, and that I am carrying it along swiftly, as though I have become the messenger for what is going on inside of me. Several things flash through my mind: the boy in the wallpaper, the gooseberries, that moment when the bucket pulled me under, the lost heifer, the mattress weeping, the third light. I think of my summer, of now, mostly of now.

As I am rounding the bend, reaching the point where I daren't look, I see him there, putting the clamp back down on the gate, closing it. His eyes are down, and he seems to be looking at his hands, at what he is doing. My feet batter on along the rough gravel, along the strip of tatty grass in the middle of our lane. There is only one thing I care about now, and my feet are carrying me there. As soon as he sees me he stops and grows still. I do not hesitate but keep on running towards him and by the time I reach him the gate is open and I am smack against him and lifted into his arms. For a long stretch, he holds me tight. I feel the thumping of my heart, my breaths coming out then my heart and my breaths settling differently. At a point, which feels much later, a sudden gust blows through the trees and shakes big, fat raindrops over us. My eyes are closed and I can feel him, the heat of him coming through his good clothes. When I finally open my eyes and look over his shoulder, it is my father I see, coming along strong and steady, his walking stick in his hand. I hold on as though I'll drown if I let go, and listen to the woman who seems, in her throat, to be taking it in turns, sobbing and crying, as though she is crying not for one now, but for two. I daren't keep my eyes open and yet I do, staring up the lane, past Kinsella's shoulder, seeing what he can't. If some part of me wants with all my heart to get down and tell the woman who has minded me so well that I will never, ever tell, something deeper keeps me there in Kinsella's arms, holding on.

'Daddy,' I keep calling him, keep warning him. 'Daddy.'

Living in Unknown

Mary Leland

The Shortlist Citation

An elegant and harrowing story of aging and reconciliation and compassion, and of the edgy separation of one's self from the moorings of past, parents and youth. This story is intense with experience and with language that's vividly apt. The reader's own experience is of an anguish that somehow consoles and preserves.

—**Richard Ford**

Author's note:

This short story grew from work in progress on a novel; while drafting these personalities and half-submerged events into a larger narrative it seemed as if they could come together with some coherence in a more condensed treatment. That was tried, it seemed to work after tidying and re-reading and re-drafting. I like these characters and the way they evince (at least I hope they evince) the commonplace if confusing experiences which can define life's major changes, often recognised only retrospectively. These people are caught in interconnecting transition: one from employment to redundancy, one from sanity to senility, others from a semi-ruling commercial class to an amorphous society in which minority differences dissolve or, like Maeve in the story, moving into a bright territory enabled by widowhood. They all still have a role in the novel, but this was another way of seeing if their reality and their actions might carry a tight truth of their own.

—*Mary Leland*

'DON'T YOU REMEMBER SWEET Alice Ben Bolt?' asked Eddie Lillis. 'Sweet Alice whose hair was so brown, who wept with delight when you gave her a smile and trembled with fear at your frown?'

Ursula smiled as her father questioned her. They were ending their visit to her friend Maeve whose newly bought house, the family had agreed, might divert him for a while. Anyway it was Ursula's turn for Eddie's outing and so far, so far, her friends had been welcoming and Maeve, whose voice when she said 'weekend' had a professional parentheses in it, had been generous with her time and with her patience. Ursula reminded herself, as she had to do so often these days, that Maeve had known Eddie Lillis before he was stricken; her affection was not forced although at times it might be forgetful. But not today. Eddie had enjoyed his visit and perhaps this purchase of an old house close to the sea had excavated something of his memory, his actual lived-in memory. He knew, or said he knew, Maeve herself, and for a little link of time it even seemed that he remembered the Conways, their stables, and Major Conway riding out every morning through the village street.

Now Ursula wondered if perhaps they had asked him to remember too much.

'In an old churchyard in the valley, Ben Bolt, in a corner obscure and alone—God! Ursula! Watch it!'

He made a frenzied clutch on the strap of his seat belt with both his hands, like a parachuter, amateur and terrified.

'It's all right, Dad. The car in front of me stopped suddenly, I had to brake. But it's okay, you can relax, I'm not going to make an end of you yet.'

'That's the one thing I'd really hate, you know, Ursula. A sudden death. I'd really hate that.'

He settled back in the seat, folding his hands in his lap again. This was now the way he ended a conversation, this physical cupping and twining of his hands. Except that it never was the end, something kept going in his head. Ursula thought about sudden death. It took a year, the saying was, to get over a death, a bereavement. This is our year, she thought, our summer to summer, from this year to next. The Irish toast, that we may be alive when this time comes round again, started into her mind. From here on, she wondered, what awaits us in this coming year?

'Oh, I don't know, Dad. Is there such a thing as a sudden death when you're eighty?'

Give him his due—which Ursula always tried to do— Eddie Lillis laughed. You could never tell what tickled him but she knew that somewhere in there was a submerged satisfaction that he had reached eighty. He was a changed man when he went to a funeral: alert but silent, exuding polite satisfaction, the last to leave when the undertakers indicated that the coffin was to be closed and that only the immediate family should remain. Ursula rather enjoyed going to funerals with him, provided they were not of people she really cared about. She liked the subversion of his very presence, the way he presented himself to the mourners.

In the car he said: 'They have laid down a slab of the granite so grey and sweet Alice lies under the stone.'

'If you had an air,' said Ursula, 'you could sing that.'

'Could you really?' Eddie Lillis asked. 'Could you really?' He was taken with the idea, and seemed content for a few moments more, a few more miles.

Then: 'Why are you stopping, Ursula?' he asked.

'Traffic lights, Dad,' said Ursula, remembering how bad his sight was now.

'I always hated those things,' he said. 'Hated having to stop. Can you go on now, yourself?'

'When I get the green, Dad, I'll move on then. Any minute now.'

'Oh,' he said as they waited. 'The far Cuillins are putting love on me as step I with the sunlight for my load. If it's thinking in your inner heart the braggart's in my step you've never smelt the tangle of the isles. Have you, Ursula?'

'No.' Ursula slid the car into gear again. 'I've never been there, never gone to Scotland, although I always wanted to.'

'Who's talking about Scotland?' her father asked. 'Was that woman talking about Scotland?' He was indignant, as if some forbidden subject had been brought irresponsibly to light.

Ursula knew he meant Maeve. 'Do you mean Maeve? No, Dad. I think she was talking about the people you used to know who lived in her house. Before she bought it.'

'She bought the house? Why did she buy the house?'

'She's got a very good job now, at the university. So she sold the house she was living in…'

'Ursula! Get around that car! Move it—get away from him the old sluggard! Go on, girl! Give him a run for his money!'

The car ahead of them was pulling sadly into the slow lane, a shudder running through its frame from a sudden puncture. Tempted to offer help, Ursula was absolved by the presence of a couple of men in the car with the woman who was driving.

She spurred ahead sharply, accelerating to appease her father's age-related appetite for pace. She noted with relief how smoothly the car responded, it was holding up well despite its years and mileage, despite her lack of faith in it. Or lack of courage—you couldn't be lackadaisical when you were taking Eddie with you. You didn't want anything to go wrong with the car then.

He had been such a good driver: patient, courteous, careful. Now he was greedy for speed, for the sensation of rapid, even dangerous, movement, of freedom from restraint. Of escape.

His hands stirred, unclasped. 'That woman who sold her house. Does she have a family?'

'Yes, Dad. A girl and two boys, but they've all left home now. That's why she sold her house and bought this one, Major Conway's one.'

'Left home? Why so? Why would they leave home?'

'They went to college in Dublin and in England, Dad. And then they got jobs away from home as well. Her daughter is in Dublin, at Trinity. They're all pretty brainy, like Maeve herself.'

'Maeve.' He pondered the name for a moment, moving his lips again over the name, wetting them with its sound.

'That Major Conway's rank was never quite certain, you know. There was some talk at the time he came home. You wouldn't remember it.'

No, she hadn't been born, thought Ursula, as she acknowledged her father's memory admonishing her own. He must have seen the rueful quirk of her mouth.

'You don't remember. He went off as a Catholic officer, you know. Family tradition and all that. When he came home he was great friends with the rectory. I was young at the time but I remember at the tennis club, they said the pope was quaking.'

That would have been a joke, but Eddie wasn't smiling.

'A strange man, the Major. If he was a major. Who's to know? I don't even know where he's living now.'

'Ah, Dad—he's been dead a long time.'

'Yes. Perhaps. I don't know. So much can't be known. There's that woman living in his house—does she have a husband, Ursula?'

This was all tedious, question after question. But Ursula was pleased with the sequence he was keeping. He still had her own name, for instance. And he was sticking with the Maeve topic too, holding his ideas together through the ghostly adhesive of Major Conway, if he had been a major.

'Yes, Dad. She did have a husband, but he died.'

Oh Col, she thought, Col in the past tense, dear Col, not a sudden death, not eighty, but death all the same.

'Did she wear black, Ursula? Did she stay indoors? You know—' and he half-turned in his seat to look more directly

61

at her. 'You know when a husband died a wife wore all black for six months—or a year. You don't see that much now. And men wore a black diamond on the coat sleeve. Well, some of them did, the Catholics. We always, always, wore a black tie. You don't see them now, I don't see them.

'Where are we now?' He lurched to attention. A town was sliding past them. A building which looked like a church, big and grey at the curve of a street.

'Dear Lord and Father of mankind, forgive our foolish ways,' he said. 'Re-clothe us in our rightful mind, in purer lives Thy service find, in deeper reverence, praise—'

'In deeper reverence, praise,' rejoined Ursula before she could stop herself and anyway liking the hymn. 'We're just going through Castlemartyr, Dad. We'll be home soon.'

'Talking about getting married—wasn't there a boy around the home place after one or other of you girls, was his name Brendan?'

It was inevitable, really, on a trip like this, any journey at all in fact could spring this kind of renewed reminiscence from her father's vapourous mind. Ursula hated it—all the family hated it, and what must it be like for her mother!—when he had to be told, and re-told, old or sad or bad news, all the stored survived griefs to be revisited.

'Yes, Dad, there was a boy called Brendan.'

'What happened to him—did he ever get married?'

Where had all this come from? The hymn might have prompted it, the verses sung at weddings.

'Yes, Dad, he did.'

'Who did he marry? If I'm not prying?'

'He married me, Dad.'

Eddie Lillis let this information float back into his brain and waited for the right response to float out.

'And did you have a nice wedding? I think your mother always wanted a proper wedding?'

The way he said it left open the possibility that Joyce Lillis had wanted a proper wedding of her own.

'Yes, Dad. We had a proper wedding, and it was very nice.'

'Was I there?' Sometimes it was heart-wrenching, he could sound suddenly uncertain, as if he knew he could not remember things which might be important. Events which had him in them, as if he were waiting to hear the narrative of his life from others.

'Indeed you were there, Dad. Sure we couldn't have had it without you.'

'Did I pay for it?' He was keenly interested now. He had never lost his grasp of money, of calculations and compounds, much as he could still produce a word for a crossword clue.

'Indeed you did. You did everything just right, just the way it should be.'

He stroked his hands as they lay folded in his lap. Glancing quickly sideways at him, Ursula saw the small rewarding smile on his lips. He was still such a handsome man, with the curly hair a brilliant silver, the heavy eyebrows still with their trace of black, the eyes still brightly brown. He was thin, and she knew his face had grown thinner, the cheeks sunken. But he had colour in his face, and character. When he and her mother went out together, as they still did frequently even if only to church, they made a handsome couple, she with her sturdy small figure so smartly dressed, her face softly pretty

63

despite its age, or pretty in a way that belonged to her age. And she was proud of him, proud to be with him even though, she had confessed to her children, she lived half in dread of what he might, or might not, do.

'And then what happened?' asked Eddie Lillis, bored by the swooping green on the banks of the road, by Ursula's law-abiding driving. 'Whatever became of him?'

Him? What him? Oh—it was Brendan.

'He went to England, Dad.' A sentence to cover an episode of years. They would be through all this again, Ursula knew. And there was a fear in her heart too: driving with her sister Rose or her brother Dermot he might ask—'Whatever became of that girl Ursula?'

'By the way,' Eddie said now, 'did I ask you how are you fixed for money?' The question came out of his contentment. She had achieved that much at least.

'I'm fine, Dad,' she lied. 'At the moment—but hold on to your spare cash, Emily will be home next week and she'll be glad of anything you have for her.'

'Emily?' His hands began to bunch, his fingers interlocked.

'My girl. She's away at school, that's why you don't see her so often, it's no wonder you forget.'

As she pressed the accelerator just that little bit harder Ursula felt the swell under her heart. My girl Emily will be home next week. She'll be home and she's been offered a place in college in England, her teachers think she should take the Cambridge offer, nothing to lose they said, and how well she would do there, how well it would suit her!

'Emily?' Eddie Lillis asked again. 'Still at school?' It was his way of anchoring himself, however briefly. There were several grandchildren of unimaginable ages all over the place.

'Nearly finished now, Dad. Her final examinations are next year. Then perhaps she'll go on to college.'

They sped on, the road running smoothly in its green-bordered, white-ribboned line. Another village spliced to the highway, its signs indicating its closeness to the city.

'What's that notice say? A house for sale? And another one—another house for sale? Two houses for sale in the same street?'

Ursula had gone past so quickly she hadn't had time to see. Her peripheral vision wasn't good enough for many drives with her father who saw everything slant-ways or diffused. For a second she hesitated, almost stopping; this distraction happened so often she should not be disturbed by it, she should be able to drive on without an inflection in the rhythm. It was so much better than his rage at traffic signals, his zest for speed.

'When,' said Eddie Lillis, his voice becalmed and questioning, 'in thy dreaming, moons like these shall shine again, and daylight beaming prove thy dreams are vain, wilt thou not, relenting, for thine absent lover sigh? In thy heart consenting to a prayer gone by?'

There was a song, now, thought Ursula. There was a song. Like O'Casey—a darlin' song. A song of Sunday evening card games, aunts and uncles at the big table, her mother judicious with the sherry and the lovely wedding-present glasses out of the china cabinet, the sandwiches, crustless and cut thin as the playing cards, waiting under damp tea towels in the kitchen.

We all graduated to those evenings, Ursula remembered.

We all got our place at that table, our turn to deal, to call, to wager. And how good they were to us, how willing before they got going with the Whist and One Hundred and Ten to play Snap with us, or Sevens, or even, especially for me, Memories. All I was good at.

And then we went upstairs when we were still little, and heard through the floorboards of our bedrooms Daddy's voice—*In thy dark eyes' splendour, where the warm light loves to dwell, weary looks, yet tender, speak a fond farewell*—and then all the voices joining in: *Nita, Juanita, ask thy soul if we should part; Nita, Juanita, lean thou on… my… heart.* We could tell the voices: Uncle Denis, Uncle Bob, Aunty Kitty—not a single one of them a blood relation.

'Did I ask you how you're off for money?' Eddie Lillis had found sanctuary again. 'I worry about you, you know. How's that job of yours going?'

Going—going—gone. That job of yours. He had never really believed in that job of hers. The job at the Arts Centre. That was when he was completely well, completely himself. Only a few years ago.

How good it was that he had blanked out his disgust when Brendan left, when those sad days brought him to visit her with angry fatherly concern morning and evening, inducing a walk, a drive—those gentle outings when he was in the full of his health! The times he reminded her that he was only too willing to help in any way he could, pressing bundles of banknotes into her resisting hands, only waiting, he said, for her permission before ringing someone he knew in an office, in a school, to see if there was some nice little place for her.

For all she knew he had made those telephone calls. For all she knew, and she knew enough to suspect this, he had made those calls and they had been repulsed. Nicely, of course. Without rancour, but without regret too. It was what was happening in the world of Eddie and Joyce Lillis: it was only when it began to change that Eddie and people like him realised that they belonged to an old order. The known contours of their world had shifted, leaving them not so much behind as on the undefined margins of the new establishment.

He had never believed in the arts. Despite Nita, Juanita and the fading orthodoxy of his grammar school education. He had never accepted her decision to leave her part-time teaching job for the full-time arts administration post which to Ursula and to her mother and to all her friends seemed so ideal, so right, for her. His doubt had been prophetic, their certainty had been betrayed.

So when she most needed her father's help Ursula could not have it. She had the support of her mother, who tried to juggle the forecast of Eddie's future with the needs of Ursula's present existence although she too had sighed an acceptance of avenues now closed to her.

It's all juggling, thought Ursula, who believed she didn't envy Maeve a bit. While she had waited for her father to finish in Maeve's bathroom—Eddie loved bathrooms, they offered a kind of security, you couldn't be caught short in a bathroom—she sat in the car with the windows down, Maeve herself framed in the hall door where she watched to make sure Eddie would not lose his way.

There was a little driveway to Maeve's house, and trees shading the gravel, lovely trees, an evergreen oak and some limes and birches and a small stand of rowans. Ursula told her what they were. Maeve wasn't too sure of their identity, but she didn't gloat, now that she had them.

Her offer of money to help out, a term-less unsecured loan, had been so delicately made that it was painful to refuse as Ursula had refused it. They had smiled and kissed, and Ursula's obstinacy had been a kind of absolution for Maeve, releasing her to enjoy what she had won for herself.

You couldn't envy Maeve. If things had come right for her they had come right as a kind of restoration. Sitting in the car, watching the sunny shadows on the gravel, Ursula saw Maeve framed as if forever in the white substantial arch of the doorway, the red and yellow tiles stretching behind her as the hall faded into the house's centre. It was as if Col had never been; there was no shadow of him in the recesses beyond the door. He lived, if he lived at all, in the past and yet Ursula thought of him now, a simple absence, a loss, forever outside this new world his death had allowed for Maeve.

When she turned the key in the ignition to make sure it would start immediately Eddie got in the car the engine shrilled and whined and died. Ursula pulled out the choke. Again it whined, and she jabbed at the accelerator, thinking press not pump but Jesus! Come on! She couldn't say anything like that in Eddie's hearing; Protestants had no curses.

In the doorway Maeve groaned; she called out—'I can't stand this!' and turned back into the house.

Ursula tried again, the engine caught and the car settled to a low purring. Maeve came back with her hand on Eddie's arm. When he was seated and strapped in she patted the roof of the car.

Ursula said, ruefully, but smiling—'Why is it that other people's cars always seem to start at once?'

Maeve didn't smile. 'They have better cars, Ursula,' she said.

She didn't have to say that. It was obvious. It wasn't what Ursula needed to hear.

That was like Maeve these days. Her smart Volvo was around the back: the house had a garage—formerly a coach-house, said Maeve, who was not gloating—as well as its short curved drive, its trees which acted like a slatted sounding board for the sea.

It was a second-hand Volvo, small, but not old. Maeve had bought it when the college job was confirmed. When everything began to come together and the pattern of her accepted future was set. The boys graduated and post-graduated and took jobs in London. Moya was close to graduation in Dublin. It was a kind of treaty, the defining of a recognisable landscape to which Maeve now had her own key.

'Traffic calming' said the sign, hatched in red.

'What's that sign! What's that sign!' Eddie had jumped out of his doze and pushed himself upright in his seat.

When he was subdued again Ursula regained her thoughts of Maeve. It was odd that, when she considered it, she could place this definite-ness in Maeve to something other than the new job. The new job had been planned for, plotted. When, after all the pain of Col's dissolution, Maeve had discovered that the insurance payout meant she would not have to go back to work immediately, she decided instead to go back to university. An additional degree, and then a doctorate and then a year of teaching in America. But this wasn't just recovery, there had been a kind of reconstruction. As if Maeve had been re-making herself. She had been so focused. So intent, as though her sadness should not be wasted; instead it had solidified and become purpose. Perhaps, Ursula thought now as the yellow strips fled under her wheels, Maeve had been able to think of the future after all. Even when it was so black and bleak and nothing other than the time she had had to endure before the future would arrive.

Am I focused? I have had grief too. But I had no insurance. That'll be the next thing, insurance against marriage breakdown, like a three-year guarantee on the return of wedding presents.

Eddie was asleep beside her. The car was like a little travelling cell containing both of them. Nucleii. Pinheads of potential. It had been a day of clouds but now with the evening the sun struck out, its rays sudden, hot, amber, catching her eyes sideways on as though something splashed brightly in a corner of her vision.

What am I going to do?

She had not asked Maeve, although she had thought, when arranging the journey, that she would ask her. Maeve had already tried to help by finding temporary teaching work which had kept Ursula in what Maeve called a network. But there was a briskness about Maeve these days. As though she would only talk to the point. She used phrases like 'on message', even 'the same hymn sheet'. That definite-ness.

Ursula suspected she knew when it began, for it was new. It was new in its constancy, anyway.

It began with Mount Conway. Someday she might tell Maeve of Eddie's doubts about the Major. But it was true: Maeve was concentrated on her life. Seeing her arrive home from the supermarket with her orderly purchases, the toilet paper in eight-roll packs to match the colour of the upstairs bathroom—itself complete to a little hunted-for knocker on the door—and of the downstairs loo, Ursula understood more clearly than ever before that for Maeve there were now few incidentals.

This was a contrast which made Ursula feel herself to be incidental. Look at her here, now, with a father who in ten minutes' time would not remember her name or who she was. Even Emily, her Emily, would be leaving home within this coming, weighted year. She remembered Emily's first departure for boarding school, its tears and bewilderment. As parents she and Brendan were just clearing the ground, getting the child out of the way, making a space in which they could finalise their combat. And the child knew it. Once the ground was cleared it seemed to disappear from beneath their feet although so much remained—the house, the school fees, their separate families set at a distance, their church—going abandoned.

A wave of worry flushed over her body as she remembered all she had to do. In this wake of familiar panic amounting almost to nausea, Ursula's skin prickled. Menopause. A word with meaning. A cessation of blood—God, she was glad of that at least!

'They have raised up a slab of granite so grey,' murmured Eddie Lillis from his seat beside her. 'And sweet Alice lies under the stone.'

Sweet Alice must have been something of a nuisance, thought Ursula. Supine even when alive. But she couldn't help wondering at the same time if it should be fitted a slab.

The sun flared across the windscreen. Ursula pulled the visor down, dulling the glare. All this is making me sour, she reflected as she came to the first set of lights that would now impede her progress through the city. Sour, and hot. Slowing, she recognised the undertow of anxiety, something resting there under her rib cage, something spurting a corrosive foretaste of regrets to come.

Eddie Lillis roused himself, unclasping the seat belt.

'I hate these bloody things!' he said, gesturing at the lights. 'They're always red—I don't know how you put up with it!'

He lunged forward, his left hand going to the door-handle. Ursula, about to move off, shoved her foot on the brake and stretched out her arm to catch him, to hold him back, terrified he was going to hurl himself out of the car.

'Let me go!' he shouted, 'I'm only going to turn off the lights—they shouldn't be on this way when you're trying to get home!'

'Dad!' she gasped, clutching his arm, the coarse tweed scratching her palm. 'Dad! We've got the green! It's all right, we're on our way!'

He sat back with a smile of triumph. Shaking, Ursula got away just as the lights changed again. She could feel her heart thumping below her neck, it hurt her, she wanted to stroke the skin there, to loosen it.

Had there been anyone behind her? She had not had time to look, not even in the wing mirror. He had seemed so determined to jump out, she had got such a fright! The car ground its way across the bridge and over the old sunken railway tracks as if it too were trembling. She tried to plot the way back to her parents' house so as to avoid any more traffic lights; it was impossible.

She felt the sting of vomit in her throat, the taut throb that meant a headache. She longed for her own bedroom, the white pillows, the comfort she arranged for herself, its solitariness. Her home.

Her mother saw nothing wrong. Eddie, Joyce could see, had had a lovely time. Joyce herself had had a lovely time, visiting an old friend, unworried for hours, time like a few precious coins in her lap to be spent at her own will.

She had made plans for tennis, she told Ursula in the hallway as Eddie fumbled his way upstairs. Rose had rung to say there was a funeral Eddie would enjoy and after that she could stay with him until she had to collect the children from school. That would give Joyce three entire unbroken hours. Her face shone as she offered the timetable to reassure Ursula. She did not notice Ursula's dimmed smile, she did not wonder that Ursula refused her offer of a cup of tea.

They stood in the hall, the dog Paddy running back downstairs after following Eddie as far as the bathroom. He jumped at Ursula, thrusting his nose into her hand, his wiry body curving around her legs. His thick coarse hair reminded her of the feel of her father's jacket when she grasped it in the car. She felt she was going to faint.

They heard Eddie shouting. 'Can I forget you, or will my heart remind me that once we walked in a moonlit dream? Can I forget you, when everything reminds me how sweet you made the moonlight seem?'

Paddy bounced back up the stairs, his tail whacking the banisters as he raced towards his master's voice. Joyce laughed, a loud clear unencumbered sound that amazed Ursula, and then cheered her. She kissed Joyce. She said in their shorthand for significant messages—'I've no news, I'm still waiting to hear more about that curatorship but I'm not betting on anything coming from it. I'll phone as soon as I have anything to tell you.'

As she left she heard her father open an upstairs window. He shouted after her, as if in farewell: 'Will the glory of your nearness fade as moonlight fades in a veil of rain? Can I forget you, or will my heart remind me how much I want you back again?'

She heard the window shut with a thud. She drove out of the sunny suburban enclave aiming for home as if she could get there on automatic pilot. She would, she would, she would fill in the forms for the American visa. This morning's late post had brought nothing; no notice of when the redundancy money would be lodged, no indication from the employment agency as to whether or not the file she had given them had been found, no response to either of the two applications she had made—in one case over a month ago—for appointments in regional arts administration. No answer to her application for a curatorship in Dublin.

She hadn't been idle. She had tried, was still trying to make the telephone ring, the email respond. There had been interviews: encouraged into it by friends and former colleagues, encouraged to seek a job which, they said, had been made for her—much as they had said before. It had been sordid—that was her word for it as she tried to cast it out of her memory. Sordid. A meeting with junior executives in a publishing company boardroom. They hadn't read her CV, they said, they could take it for granted knowing her so well. What were her ideas, they asked, explaining that they'd continue with the interview even though one of their number was in the jacks, he'd be along in a minute. As indeed he had been, still zipping, still pushing his shirt ends into a too-tight waistband.

She knew that they were getting their obligation to her friends out of the way, this was not a real interview and she would not get the job. She didn't open her folder or disclose her ideas to them but sat there, not smiling, waiting for them to ask the questions which were meant to expose her unsuitability for the short list.

She saw her hands on her portfolio and thought as she noticed again her pink nail-polish that at least she hadn't spent any money on preparing for this, buying nothing more than a new pair of tights.

Nothing bad was happening here, nothing other than a familiar dishonesty, nothing that wasn't happening to many others just like Ursula. There was no reason why she should feel like a tart, a harlot. Yet she did. Strutting her stuff she had been, painting her nails to beg for work.

What had she done wrong? What did other women do if this misfortune hit them? Like an accident, it had been, like a car crash. It hadn't got her down. Not yet. But it was unbalancing her, making her both fearful and fierce, afraid to try, furious in her attempts. She sought an equilibrium, longing to achieve again the symmetry of a hanging day, of a varnishing day, the adjustments of money and people, the geometry of the presentation of paintings, the way time and space were measured, the way rooms even empty of viewers could shine and beckon and be known to her and people like her, people of her ilk.

The social welfare office with its queues of explanations was next: yes, there was the little lurch of fear again, that quickly thrown stone into the pool of her life. Joyce had said that no one in their family had ever seen the inside of a welfare office. Ursula didn't tell her what it was like: the prams, the multitudes of children, the damp smell even on fine days. The unexpected embarrassed faces. The curt and inadequate cubicles, the codes, the supplications. Waiting for her dole she had comforted herself with the word: dole, and with it had come thoughts of Col's bedside and his repeating, when she appeared with flowers, the old advice to buy hyacinths to feed the soul. 'With the dole,' he had said, giving the word its old meaning, something left over, the change. Well, perhaps not so old, perhaps not inappropriate in this exchange, we are all left over, we ourselves are the dole.

Ursula's cheque was minimal—but at least it went to her bank account. She need only present herself in person once a month. A monthly appearance; she felt like the woman in the bible who was cursed with an issue of blood. A visitation. Something she could not welcome or make her own or accept as part of her life, not like periods which used to give her a cyclic and comforting rhythm. This was alien, something she must either conquer or escape.

She had shown yesterday's letter to Maeve: it was from her trade union, asking for more information about her circumstances, about the arrangements she had made for others working with her who were already part-time staff, about her immediate prospects.

'At the moment,' the letter said, 'our records show that you are working in Unknown.'

Maeve had said to hold on, hold on. Summertime meant there would be no regular teaching opportunities but there might be something at a summer school. Hold on, she had said, stick around. You never know.

Hold on to what? Holding on meant staying still. Despite the terrors, the fears for Emily and their warm whispered plans for her future, Ursula had never felt so impelled to movement, to action, to making things happen. Like Eddie Lillis. Now she felt the impulse again: it was the pressure of desperation, the crunching pang which kept her sitting in her car outside her own front door as if to catch her breath in readiness for the next, the next and then the next effort again.

In the sanctuary of her hall Ursula smelled the mist of the life she had lived here. With Brendan, with Emily. Tile, plaster, paint and paper, carpet and lampshade, picture and chair. Photograph. Her gallery. She remembered the union's letter trembling in her hand: I'm not working in unknown, she thought. I'm living in unknown. Keep breathing, she told herself. Think of the visa. Think of America. Can I forget you when everything reminds me?

This Isn't Heaven

Molly McCloskey

The Shortlist Citation

A subtle and perceptive story, set in contemporary Africa, that deftly and affectingly compresses and focuses time and geography. Its signal success is one that it shares with many excellent stories: to locate drama to the side of where we might expect to find it and then to make its subject seem essential. Here, a man loves a woman, but never manages to experience love at all.

—Richard Ford

Author's note:

For a year and a half, I worked for an office of the United Nations that was concerned with coordinating humanitarian assistance for Somalia. The office was based in Kenya, but everyone travelled, with varying degrees of frequency, in and out of Somalia. The story grew out of that experience. One of the things that interested me about that time was the question of what kept people working in dangerous and difficult places—I mean the people who had a choice, who could've had lucrative jobs in safe, stable environments—and how people tended to present their own motivations. I tried to trace, in the three characters, the arc of feeling that people experience working in such a context: from early idealism to cynical burn-out and what lies in between. And, I wanted to tell an intimate story, one of unrequited—or perhaps misguided—love(s), because even in the midst of large tragedies, we fall back on our own personal dramas.

—*Molly McCloskey*

I HAD COME TO MEET HER off the plane from Kenya, the day she took up her post. Though I'd seen her before, I knew little about her. Certainly, she hadn't struck me as remarkable, or no more remarkable than the scores of other young women I'd worked with. She was coming for a two-year stint in what's known as the deep field, an expression that always smacked of some collective self-regard. The airstrip was in the south of the country, where things were bad. After a few meetings here, we would head north, to relative stability, to the self-declared autonomous republic, a phrase that also smacked of self-regard.

The south had been my first posting, twelve years earlier. I'd been other places since—Asia and the Balkans—but had come back here a year ago, much water, and a marriage, under the bridge. As I sat waiting for her at the airstrip, I thought about my own first arrival here. How I had expected, on looking down from the plane, to see something like a scene from *Ben Hur*—strife everywhere, people running hither and thither in the pillowing clouds of dust raised by pockets of combat. The scene repeated over and over across the landscape, as though I were looking down on a vast studio in which several war movies were being shot at once. Instead, I saw goats scattering like slow sparks in all directions and brown arid fields divided into careful squares. I saw miles and miles of emptiness.

Not much had changed in a dozen years. The clans were still playing out their absurdist dramas. The droughts, the floods, the locusts, the plagues of cholera and malaria were all still in evidence. What changes there were seemed mostly to be within ourselves, emissaries from the world beyond, arriving in wavelets with our trail mix and our ever sleeker Macs and our international conventions.

That day, there was the usual clutch of aid workers slouched on the concrete benches in what we referred to as the departure lounge, a cement porch on which stringy old men sold souvenirs—coins from the old colonial powers, milk gourds, jewellery. Beyond the perimeter of the airstrip was a sea of polystyrene, plastic bags that had snagged themselves on thorny shrubs. A dry wind was blowing in gusts, causing the bags to inflate, periodically, like lungs.

The plane was an hour late, and as the hatch opened I wondered for a moment if I'd even recognise her. I knew that we'd been at the same meetings a handful of times in Nairobi. We had nodded at one another—a kind of tribal recognition, we were both from Ireland—the non-greeting the bureaucracy bred, infused with guardedness, a subtext of something vaguely sexual, overlaid with the neuroses of rank and experience. But for a moment, I couldn't summon her face.

When she stepped out, I immediately remembered her, though it was also as if I were seeing her for the first time. For a long while afterwards, every time I saw her, I saw, like an after-image, the way she looked that day, crossing the airstrip on a windy afternoon, her lank brown hair escaping the desultory head scarf, a figure framed by the slanting saplings that marked the airstrip's border.

Marie was just gone thirty. This was her first posting. She'd worked as a dogsbody at an NGO in Dublin, then taken her postgrad in the UK. One of those human rights theory degrees that weren't yet *de rigueur* when I had started out. Apart from a holiday in Costa Rica, she'd never been out of Europe before her arrival in Nairobi six weeks before. Now she had left the relative safety of car jackings and random shootings and landed in one of the most dangerous countries on Earth.

I asked her if Kenya had been what she'd expected, and she answered me with an unembarrassed honesty I liked. She had, I would learn, a strange kind of confidence that seemed to come not from anything she'd done but from knowing, already, that to pretend was to waste time. Pretending was not what we were here for.

'To be honest,' she said, 'I expected the *Night of the Living Dead*.'

We were riding in the back of the Land Cruiser, heading to the office so she could meet her colleagues in the south. She scratched her forehead and glanced in the direction of the driver, who spoke English but was listening to a jangly discordant cassette. 'You know,' she continued, 'the city rife with HIV, skeletal figures everywhere. I'd read the HIV rate was over thirty percent in some areas of the country, and I kept imagining walking down the street and these cadaverous figures streaming past. Like in *Night of the Living Dead*.'

I was tempted to say something wise and knowing—about Western attitudes to Africa, attitudes in which I would pretend to implicate myself, while making clear I was long since free of such ignorance. But something about her caused the impulse to fall away. Anyway, I wondered were her imaginings so far from reality. How many times had I driven these streets and seen the listlessness with which people drifted through the day? How many thousands of days had I seen people sitting by the side of the road, doing nothing, for hours on end. Not because they were dying, but because there was nothing to do, and even if there was, there was little point in doing it. It was one of the things that still had the capacity to surprise me— how much of the world passed its day doing nothing at all.

'I don't think I've ever seen that film,' I said.

We weren't in the same office but were working on the same project—monitoring the yearly migration of tens of thousands of people who came to the north of the country to cross the Gulf of Aden to Yemen, and trying to figure out how to keep them from dying while they were doing it. They came mostly from the Oromo, Tigrinya and Somali regions of Ethiopia, and from the south of Somalia itself, paying smugglers up to a hundred and fifty dollars a shot to take them across the Gulf. The business was so profitable that competing smugglers pooled funds to buy a new boat if one sank or was captured by the Yemeni coastguard. It was a rare instance of communal spirit.

Along the transit routes, the migrants were subject to everything from snake bites and hypothermia to extortion and rape. They had to dodge police, petty officials, random armed militia and common criminals. Then there was the crossing. If the smugglers sensed danger, they just dumped their passengers overboard, and some would swim ashore and some would drown and some would fall victim to sharks.

Marie and I travelled back and forth between the two cities of the north—Hargeisa, one of the transit points, and Bossaso, where the port was—trying to find out everything we could. Some days it seemed like all we would have at the end of our labours was another report. And that nothing we would do or say or learn would matter. Everybody knew that. The production of reports was also a profitable business.

For a long time, I wasn't in love with her. It was more that I saw myself in her, in some early, unadulterated form. Back when I had arrived in such places with an appetite for ambiguity, and the energy to fine-tune my understanding. When I felt the kind of earnest respect one feels for a stern challenge. As though it could all be put right if only we applied ourselves with sufficient purpose and rationality. In turn, I'd expected to be changed. I was prepared to have my worldview upended. I regarded the sites of famine and conflict and displacement as if they were places of pilgrimage that would reveal, in a flash, something ultimate and true to me, slicing my life into a before and an after.

Marie had that kind of awe. She'd grown up in a house where on the mantel, amongst the family photos of trips to the Blaskets and Cape Clear (her father was an island-lover), was a grainy photo taken in Yola, in Northern Nigeria, in the late sixties. It was of her aunt, who'd been a Sister of Mercy. Though she made allowances for the historical context, Marie didn't approve of missionary work. What impressed her was the paradox of this small and gentle woman who was unafraid of deprivation, or the smell of rotting flesh, or the superstitions that surrounded her.

Marie came here knowing far more than her aunt had. The internet and television had rendered everything familiar. The photos on her laptop were all high-resolution. There was no mistaking that she was coming to a land of cyclic starvation and pointless, petty warfare. She was coming to a failed state. And, yet, some kind of naiveté prevailed. Like a lot of essentially decent but slightly dreamy people, Marie had imagined her life here, our work, in the form of abstractions. She imagined that on a continent so vast and so fucked up, surely one could *only* do good. As though the place were an extremely messy room one looked at and thought: *where to start?* But knew that any start was better than none at all.

'When I thought of working here,' she told me, 'I used to see a line of firemen. You know, before there were fire hydrants or hoses. A line of firemen, passing buckets of water to douse the flames of a burning house, a house so big it dwarfed their efforts.'

'That's odd,' I said, and laughed. By then, I knew her well enough to laugh at such admissions.

And hubristic, I thought. Possibly offensive. Definitely far from reality. But in a way, just an abstract gloss on all the brochures and websites she'd seen, the flyers that arrived through the letter box, reminding her that ten euros could save the sight of five children. Those savagely simplistic equations that render, in a sentence, all the world's tragedies eradicable.

*

Until the bombs that shook us out of our complacency, the north of the country, where we were posted, was relatively peaceful, though our movement after dark was still restricted. We had long nights in which there was nothing at all to do but sit in our rooms talking and smoking, sipping whiskey someone had secreted over from Kenya.

One night she said, 'Tell me something you love about here.'

No one had ever asked me that before. We all took it for granted that there was nothing to love.

'Love? Well.'

'Is that a stretch?'

I bit my lip in a parody of deep thought.

'Okay,' she said. 'This isn't heaven. But there must be something.'

'Yes,' I said. 'There are a few things.'

And I listed them. I loved the redness of the soil. I loved when it rained at night and grew suddenly cold. I loved the camels, who belonged to a biblically distant time rather than to the present, with its slew of contradictions, its mud huts and its Blackberries. I loved the dik-diks that darted past and the shrub that flowered a brilliant red. I even loved the barrenness at times, the flat blank stare of the earth that was such a counterpoint to all the teeming crowded cities I had ever enjoyed or hated. I loved how quiet the world could be without piped music and car alarms. I loved the black humour, and the coloured drawings on the outer walls of shops, and how the people shouted when they talked, as though across great distances. Pastoralists through and through.

'And I love the two ostriches that live in the compound,' I said. 'You know the skin on the female's face turns bright red during mating season. You haven't been here for mating season.'

'No,' she said, and looked at me with a blatantly ironic coyness. 'I haven't.'

We talked about work, too. About our colleagues. About what we had seen that day, or that week, when we'd travelled to the port. About the latest accusations of collusion between government officials and smugglers. We marvelled at the ingenuity of the smugglers—they knew how to market themselves and used agents in Mogadishu and elsewhere to scout for them. They could arrange transport from the most unpromising corners of nowhere. They also, like the snake-oil salesmen that they were, lied to people about the risks of the journey and hyped what awaited them in Yemen. It might've been a little rough around the edges but, given the country's non-existent infrastructure, the operation was run with an impressive efficiency. And we asked ourselves, for the thousandth time, what might the country be like if all that resourcefulness was put to more salubrious use. We told each other the stories we ourselves had been told, by people who'd seen friends drowned or beaten or raped right in front of them. Who, though they knew it was wrong, accepted it all as part of the life they'd been born into. People who wanted nothing more than to leave this place, this place that we—whether for money or adventure or a compassion nurtured by fund-raising flyers—had chosen to be.

And we talked about ourselves, about our families, our childhoods, our first loves. We told intimate stories, the way you do in such outbacks. I told her about my marriage to Suzanne, before we drifted apart and I ended up back in East Africa, the strange cosiness of our life in a corner of the

Balkans, after the war, when Suzanne had been seconded and come from Ireland to join me. I told her of the garbage and the packs of dogs and the cold that was like nothing I'd ever felt before, of how as filthy and as angry as the place was, it was the richest time of our life together.

She told me about her mother falling in love with a family friend, the scandal of it when she'd left her father—and at the age of fifty-three. She told me about the nightmares she had of tidal waves, about her weak backhand, and about her cousin who'd been born with a hole in his heart. She told me about college, about the grotty old movie house in Rathmines where in the back row she and her boyfriend used to ease one another to climax. A soundless, motionless, white-knuckled gratification that was not without its irony: they could've gone to his house and done it all in comfort; his parents turned a blind eye. Instead, they'd fabricated subterfuge, contriving more furtive scenarios: instinctive, last ditch attempts, only half-understood, to slow their own growing up.

Why didn't I try? She was nine years younger than I was, there was nothing implausible about it. But I made the mistake of thinking her exceptional, above the fray of human foolishness. She had (despite the grotty movie house) a kind of uprightness that made me want to be a better person. Which didn't mean a life of celibacy, but rather a way of proceeding with more dignity and wisdom than perhaps I so far had. What I was doing all those nights, with all that talking, was courting her, in the only way I thought she would accept being courted.

When she took up with him, I realised that she was just like everybody else. Not living the life I'd imagined for her, but an ordinary one, messy and tacky and occasionally embarrassing. She wanted to be the woman in the grainy photo in Yola, not a religious by any means, but someone living a life of dedication and service, a life boiled down to its essentials, free of the trappings of inherited prosperity and self-indulgence. She was expecting to surprise herself with her capacities. And I agreed to that vision. But she was also young and full of appetites, and she wanted experiences. Dramatic ones. That, I had missed. And so when it happened, I saw it as tacky and predictable. Because by then I had fallen in love with her.

He lived in Nairobi with his wife and his two twenty-something kids who had recently come to join them from Europe. He was Peruvian, a lawyer who'd lived with death threats in Lima until his wife finally said *enough*, and they fled to Spain. He looked to me like a creature you'd meet at a Dionysian revel deep in the wood. He had a trimmed grey beard and dark, wide-set eyes, and his head was covered in a thin layer of greying ringlets that I found overtly and disturbingly suggestive. I could picture him shirtless, a goat from the waist down. He had another side, too. With sunglasses and a straw hat to shield him from the sun, he resembled a South American drug dealer. I saw a photo of him at a refugee camp and he could've been someone snapped waiting at an airstrip in the jungle, someone who'd appear at the wrong end of a pointer at a DEA briefing.

She was very much in love with him. Or at least believed she was. What is the difference, really. Maybe it's only time that separates the believing from it being so. I'd see her walking through the compound, on her way to the office, or standing at the tea shops or at the edge of the slums in Bossaso, sweating and tense but strangely aglow. She looked saturated with something—energy or desire. She seemed to exist with a level of intensity I found it hard to believe others couldn't see.

Because it was a hardship station, we got one week's leave after every five in the field. Sometimes we went on safari or to the coast near Mombasa, where the rickety Masai wandered the beaches for sex, looking self-conscious and redundant. Mostly, we just went to Nairobi, for a taste of normal life. In spite of the mess that it was, I loved Nairobi. The airport had a low-slung and tropical feel to it that I never tired of. In the mornings, the light in the city was green-gold. Before rain it turned a darkening purple, and afterwards that beautiful sickly yellow. The mornings felt like spring, and evenings often like autumn. After the aridity we were used to, the deforestation and the cracked earth, the suburbs of Nairobi were so lush the earth had a drunken look to it, the gardens lurid and the flowers spilling extravagantly over high walls. When the jacaranda were in bloom, the upper limits of your horizon would be bathed in lavender and the streets were littered with lavender petals, as though they'd just been strewn for the pleasure of a passing entourage.

I kept an apartment in the suburbs. It was on the fourth floor, nearly level with the tree line. From that height, the sound of the traffic and the dogs barking was just distant enough to be homely. The breeze would come in through the windows that opened onto the balcony and sometimes, too, the smell of the sweet incense the Indians burned. Evenings, I'd sit on the balcony and listen to the call to prayer from the mosque at Eastleigh that, like the traffic, was perfectly distant and unexpectedly consoling. After a heavy rain, termite wings littered the walkway outside my door like the detritus of some natural massacre.

We passed our leave there loafing, swimming at the Holiday Inn or the Norfolk, going to dinner parties with friends at the French or Vietnamese restaurants. The tiered terraces and the soft candlelight. Between us we had seen the worst there was to see in all the earth's most wretched corners, and we tossed off references to atrocities so casually. We spoke of the more infamous despots as though they were people we had known in school. We shared a camaraderie that was reminiscent of late adolescence, only now tinged with the sense of having met on the other side of something shattering. Our lives seemed wistful and profound, and life itself had a glow of unearned nostalgia.

We were also cynical about everything that happened in the field. About the fact that we had to pay criminals at checkpoints so that convoys carrying aid for their own people wouldn't be attacked. About the fact that food was stolen and sold, or given to people it wasn't intended for, simply because they had a sliver more power. About the fact that elected officials often left the office at lunchtime, because that was when the khat-chewing began and the narcotic haze descended, while we continued working, trying to cobble their country back together again.

Somehow, in spite of everything we knew, we took our failures and our limited capacities personally. At least those of us who had come from other continents. Because however we couched it, however true our intentions, there was always the hint of a secularised missionary self-regard. Our African colleagues, from Liberia and Sierra Leone, who had so much more to be cynical about, were less so. There was a matter-of-factness, a lack of sentimentality, with which they approached atrocity, and they had a clearer view of humankind. They did their jobs and had no shame about the salary and didn't bother much with affectations about a higher calling.

*

He would often fly into the north from Nairobi, troubleshooting. Fires in the camps or looted plastic sheeting or the latest luckless hoards to be illegally detained. He'd stay at the big hotel in town—the only decent hotel in the entire country—and she'd sneak into his room. They'd be fucking and in the background, at dawn, the call to prayer would drift in. She said it felt like God was coming into the room.

'We could be stoned in the public square,' she reminded me, as though I had something to do with it. 'Sometimes I find it beautiful,' she went on, 'when it happens when we're, you know. Is that paradoxical? I should feel admonished by God and instead I feel like...' She sighed.

I felt a wave of sourness. 'Does it make it more exciting?'

She ignored the sarcasm, or missed it, and said, 'You'd think it might, the added taboo. But not at all. Isn't that odd? Maybe we're suffering from taboo fatigue. Everything we fucking do here is taboo. I feel like a walking taboo.'

I offered her a half-smile. I wanted to hear more and yet, of course, I didn't. I hardly trusted myself to say anything.

'Or maybe,' she said, 'the thought of stoning is so far

removed from our reality that we can't take the idea seriously enough to excite us. I mean *one*, one can't.' She liked nothing more than to talk about him, but often tried— maybe for my sake—to camouflage the subject amidst some psycho-cultural analysis. 'You know you can only be envious of people two steps ahead of you on the status ladder.'

'Yes,' I said with sudden relief. 'Something like that.'

She handed me a cigarette. 'Are you envious of anyone?' she asked.

The relief drained. But it was a question posed in all innocence. She really didn't know, and I wasn't sure whether to credit myself with discretion and a courtly dignity or to take it as an insult, an indication of a certain insubstantiality on my part.

In November, the rains came. The flooding in the south was biblical. People were climbing trees to escape the crocodiles, eating leaves to survive. Whole villages were submerged or cut off. The garbage and the stagnant water teemed with maggots and worms. Malaria and diarrhoea were rampant. Over 400,000 people were on the move, trying to reach food and shelter. Many came north. Some would never go home again, now that they were here. They would moulder away in another camp, along with hoards of other long-term displaced, or they would decide to make the crossing to Yemen.

Marie and I, along with two other colleagues, met with the District Commissioner about the influx. He'd had polio and one of his legs was withered and turned in, and the disfigurement was in stark contrast to his upper body, which was thick and strong. His face was handsome in a soft, full way, like someone you'd see in an African soap. He was guileless without being naive. Gentle but imposing. He probably wasn't more than thirty. Both Marie and I were extremely fond of him. We wanted to whisk him off to another world, where his intelligence and his dignity would have the kind of context they deserved.

He told us that three Somalis had died the day before, on the way to the port. They'd been travelling in the back of a lorry and had died of dehydration, their bodies dumped behind some garbage. Marie wrote it all down. We said we'd talk to the authorities in Bossaso. We'd talk to the police. We'd talk to our bosses in Nairobi. Then she and I drove back to the office together. I knew she was upset without being shocked. I had never seen her shocked, a fact she continued to attribute to the internet.

'We've seen everything virtually,' she said. 'So by the time you actually see it, it seems slightly unreal. Like going to the theatre after growing up on cinema.'

I was just old enough to not feel quite the same. By the time I had the world and all its grotesqueries at my fingertips, I was fully formed. Still, I used to wonder why the poverty had never shocked me. What had shocked me, after seeing poverty, was wealth, and the ease with which people seemed to have their money. After having lived in places where the elite hid their wealth behind high walls, the casual display of simple, middle-class material comfort offended me. Whether it was an excessive concern for security I'd acquired or some misguided moral code that said it was okay to have more as long as one pretended not to, I wasn't sure. I knew that at work, in front of the locals, we didn't compare the price of laptops or talk about skiing on our next trip to Geneva. We hid our good luck behind high walls, and it seemed to make everyone feel less uneasy.

*

When she was in Nairobi for meetings or on leave, he'd escape the office at lunch hour and meet her at the apartment of a friend of hers, where she kept a room, after which he would slink—insofar as one can slink when in a vehicle—out the gate and back up towards Chiromo Road and the office. Our world was so small that she could see him at a party that very night. He'd be with his wife, and it would be all loaded glances and elaborately choreographed avoidance.

I knew, of course, what she was going through. I knew that like the geographical spaces of our lives, affairs divided up our world into discrete compartments, strictly defined pockets of time between which there was no spillover, no lazy continuity of experience, and that this way of living made us hyper-aware of time, and transience. I knew the way another person's skin could take on the quality of temporality, so that you felt under your fingertips the way everything, eventually, slips away. I knew the sensation that came with the first encounter, the illusion of having discovered together something elemental— both grand and terrible—about the true nature of things. I knew, too, how quickly the thing grows heavy with anxiety and sorrow. How the whole arc of what you can and cannot be to someone gets compressed into a couple of hours, and how so much of what comes after is just humbling and tawdry detail. To remind us that we are anything but mythic.

I couldn't help but observe him. Because it wasn't only Marie I saw myself in. It was him, too. And if Marie looked to me like my younger self, what I saw in him was a more pronounced version of my disenchantment. It was clear to listen to him that any passion he'd had for justice, for the work he did, was spent. Whatever had driven him all those years ago in Peru to stick it out through the death threats was gone. He was thinking, like a lot of people, of his pension. He had seen how even the smallest piece of power corrupts, how a seemingly homogenous group of people with an apparently common goal will, as a first order of business, fracture into destructive hierarchies and set about silencing the weak. He had seen a district official obstructing for over a year the construction of a dozen latrines, and he'd seen little girls bleeding to death from circumcision, and there were days, I was sure, when he found it difficult to care.

As for me, I knew that I would leave this place with less guilt than I'd arrived with, and I wasn't even sure it mattered. I did my job in much the way I always had, perhaps better because freed of a certain weight that came with having illusions. I knew that people only stopped fighting when they were tired of it and that sometimes we were the greatest enablers of all. I knew, too, that cynicism was insufficient, and that its only value was in being a necessary stage on the way to something better.

Her own disillusionment came in the form of him. But not as you'd think. Not because he broke her heart. Rather because here, in the midst of so much suffering—of the one-meal-a-day and the maternal mortality and the ignorance so committed to its own perpetuation—she had fallen in love. Not with someone heroic and indefatigable but with someone who was burned out. A tired bourgeois sensualist with an apartment in Madrid and a couple of spoiled kids. And all day long, as she collected horrific tales and people lifted their shirts to show the scars of their beatings and smiled gauntly, beseeching her, she thought of him.

She had arrived here believing that the dramas surrounding her would be the main events of her life, and that her own life, with its small yearnings and dissatisfactions, would recede into a proper perspective, assuming the kind of minor dimensions she considered appropriate in the face of widespread tragedy. But what she'd thought would be her life had turned out to be mere backdrop—more dramatic perhaps than the streets of Rathmines, but wallpaper nonetheless.

She said to me one day. 'When things got very bad last week, and there was so much movement out of the south after the fighting, the first thing I thought was that it meant that he would come here soon.'

She wasn't being flippant. She was simply stating a fact about herself. And it was the kind of admission one didn't often hear. We, too, had our taboos.

The bombs went off at the end of that October, five attacks that took place within minutes of each other. The presidential palace, the Ethiopian consulate, some UN offices and offices of the local security forces. Twenty-nine people died. All foreigners were recalled to Nairobi, where we sat in security meetings and tried not to feel the pointlessness of it all. But it was undeniable that the one place we had considered safe, the one place that had been moving forward, had now sunk to the level of the rest of the country, and become a region of unpredictable and self-defeating violence. We lingered in Nairobi, restless and redundant, trying to carry on the business of aid by remote.

During those weeks, she had a lot of brief encounters with him, and then the whole thing ended abruptly when she got another post. She was going to Cambodia. She phoned me the day she got word about the job, and I stood at the roundabout outside the supermarket in a suburb of Nairobi and watched the world separate itself into discrete pieces. So that it no longer seemed a place that held me but like something hanging on the wall in front of me.

Before she hung up, she said, 'Why don't you come and visit me? We'll go to Angkor Wat.'

An old Land Rover belched black smoke and a man with a shoebox full of kittens for sale shoved them in my face.

'I've been,' I said.

There was the usual round of farewell drinks and dinners. We had our own farewell lunch, just the two of us. I thought that I might tell her then, because I couldn't think of a good reason not to. I thought of it like a going away present. But the minute she sat down, I knew I wouldn't tell her. I could see that she would only be embarrassed by the admission, and would feel the need to say something she thought consoling but that would probably, for a moment, make me hate her.

When she said, with an almost theatrical sigh, 'We spent

last night together,' I almost did hate her.

'The *whole night*?' I asked.

Apparently, he'd concocted some ridiculous tale for his wife and they'd got a hotel room. 'So, anyway,' she said, 'that's the end of that.'

'You're glad to be leaving, I guess.'

'I'm glad to be leaving. But not because of him.'

I nodded. 'It's time. It's time for me, too.'

'Yeah,' she said, and for just a moment she sounded old.

Within a few months, I was gone, too. I took some time off, went back to the west of Ireland for a while, to think about what I wanted next. I felt homesick for too many places, and yet nothing remained of them that I could go back to, even if I'd wanted to. I felt homesick for the life I'd had with Suzanne, those nights when the power would go and we'd have to sleep in the front room near the wood stove and we'd lie there by candlelight and hold each other, talking or not talking, just the creaturely comfort of it. The darkness reducing us to something quiet and undemanding.

And I missed cold. The sense of clarity that comes with frosts, with sharp winds. I missed the way the days lengthened and contracted, far from the equator, and the jaggedness of the cliffs along the shoreline. I missed home, though in the form of time as much as space.

Before I left Nairobi, I used to see him around at parties. I wasn't envious anymore. Because I could see that he was suffering. He had an air of bewilderment about him, like someone who'd been picked up wandering. I had the strange urge to speak to him, to say that I was sorry for whatever it had cost him. For he looked in those days like he'd lost a kind of life force, as if she had stolen whatever remained of his spirit.

The Road Wife

Eoin McNamee

The Shortlist Citation

An irresistible story of modern Europe—long-haul truckers, Russian prostitutes, storms at sea, flood-lit embarcaderos past midnight, pale longing—and death. The language here, the authority, the stark atmospherics are incomparable and by themselves are worth this story's brief, hectic, melancholy journey.

—Richard Ford

Author's note:

A few years ago I was at a garage on the road between Kilkeel and Rostrevor. It was Sunday morning. A 1996 BMW 3 Series with blacked-out windows and Latvian plates stopped at the garage. Two young men in heavy-metal T-shirts and their girlfriends who wore jeans and leather knee boots got out. The two girls went to the garage to buy cigarettes and the boys spread a map on the bonnet of the car.

All that summer blonde young men and women came to work in the fish factories and on the trawlers in Kilkeel, sweeping down from the Arctic Circle in high-mileage German cars.

A little while after this a lorry driver told me he'd spent several years hauling freight from another port. He told me about an Asian girl who lived in the trucks. She would be passed from an incoming rig to an outgoing one. I thought of her as a road wife.

—Eoin McNamee

COYLE FIRST HEARD ABOUT HER from another driver on the night ferry from Warrenpoint to Roscoff. It was September. The ship rose and fell. There were groans and shudders deep in the fabric of the hull as though something better left undisturbed was abroad in the holds and companionways.

Coyle and another driver called Duffy were alone in the canteen. The lights were turned down and Duffy's face was lit from the side by a portage light so that he looked like a character from an archetype of story, narrator of tales to a traveller met by night.

'I got something to keep you warm,' Duffy said. 'I got a girl in the cab. All the boys know her. She goes out in one run, comes back on another.'

'No thanks,' Coyle said.

'Suit yourself.'

There was good money to be had hauling blast-frozen fish from K to the continent and Coyle had signed up for six months. The previous August he had driven an empty container from Rotterdam to Bremen. When they opened it a week later they found a family of Chinese migrants. They had been asphyxiated in the under-ventilated container. They asked Coyle if he had noticed anything unusual on the trip but he hadn't.

He moved into the Atlantic Hotel on the outskirts of town which had been turned into a workers' hostel. There were weeds growing through the tarmac in the car park and the fencing was broken in places. There were foreign cooking smells in the corridors—the odour of things that were soused, things that were pickled. In his room there were two single beds and a sign in Cyrillic script. There was a yellow mark on the nightstand where a cigarette had burned itself out. The timber round the doorjamb was splintered and repaired.

On his first night he had lain awake listening to the clang of gantries from the ferry port, the noise of containers being loaded. He didn't see much of the other workers. They were Latvians and Estonians and Poles. Men from the old ports and estuary cities. There was a Baltic tang in the air. He spent two or three nights a week in the hostel and slept in the rig for the rest of the time. He felt a long way from home. On Friday and Saturday night there were discos in the basement of the hotel and afterwards there were broken bottles and beer cans in the car park.

When he wasn't driving he joined the workers gathered in a linoleum-floored common room to watch old martial arts films. Bruce Lee on the balls of his feet, ready for the sweeping head-high kick, the rushing dullards felled.

The next time Duffy offered the girl to him he hesitated. His wife had left him years ago but there were wan and tender accords that still bound him. In the end he arranged to pick her up at the gates of a freight yard. Rain slanted between the containers. Coyle scanned the container decals, the tares and capacities, dead weights. Reading the names of the shipping companies and freight lines. He liked being in ports at night. There was a sense of things in transit, in movement across great distances.

She looked oriental at first. She had slant Asiatic features, but her accent sounded Eastern European. He saw plenty of girls in the lorry parks and services but she didn't resemble them. The other girls had a wind-scoured, trafficked look. Coming from the frontier states, the Soviet-era apartment blocks and wide boulevards. They were the ruined children of frozen tundra cities, the defiled princesses.

She made him think of a character from the martial arts film, one of the rustling hostesses. He could imagine her in the triad-haunted narrow streets, at large in the night with pockmarked yakuza.

'You want the menu?' she asked.

'What menu?'

'What menu do you think? Start at twenty pounds.'

'I suppose you find a lot of loneliness on the road,' Coyle said.' I suppose men like me like to talk.'

'No,' the girl said, 'they like to have sex.'

He pulled into a lorry park and got into the bunk with her. For a while he felt like a teenager in a parked car. It was all textures and fabrics, trying to work your way through gaps in clothing, under waistbands. When he was eighteen he had owned a Volkswagen and had learned how to move in its utilitarian spaces, to find the erotics in the plastic-smelling velours and velcro-affixed seat covers and nubby fabrics.

He filled up with diesel at a service on the outskirts of Utrecht. She went to the toilet. He got into the cab and went through her handbag. There was change in the bottom of the bag. A tissue with lipstick on it. A packet of Paracodol. He found her passport. She was from the Republic of Moldova. He opened it. There were visas for countries he had never heard of. The stamps in blue and green pastel inks, the alien-looking scripts, swirling, serif-laden. They looked like the anthem of an ancient caliphate, desert-sung.

Her name was Nadia Hamsa. She had been born in 1979. There was a picture of her, badly printed, dark hair hanging over her face. He imagined a backstreet photo booth in some vice-ridden oriental milieu. Without really knowing what he was doing he put the passport in his pocket.

Every hundred miles or so he would pull off the autobahn and bang on the side of the customs-sealed container and wait for a reply. She never asked him why.

He dropped her off at the roundabout outside K. The next morning he went on a run to Marseilles that kept him away for a week. When he saw her again she was walking along the road in K with the Russian factory girls. She was wearing a factory worker's white coat and hairnet. He understood that by taking the passport he had stranded her there.

The Russian girls lived in wooden chalets beside the factory. They worked in the cold stores and dockside industrial units with wet concrete floors. They shelled prawns and levered the meat from crab toes with spiked instruments. They scraped the shells of molluscs. They dismantled creatures with pincers and slatted bodies and eyes on stalks. Invertebrate carcasses were stacked in crates.

The Russian girls were blonde with dark shadows under their eyes. The drivers said they were cold and emotionless but Coyle thought that they were like young women in flight from a great sin. There was a lingering taint of infanticide. The other drivers were morose, authoritarian men with moustaches and tattoos who listened to country music in their cabs.

On his evening off Coyle would walk out beyond the harbour onto the esplanade. There was a Victorian swimming baths there, built at the same time as the one in which his father had taught him to swim. There was the same cracked tiling and rusted handrails. Brackish water pooled on the broken companionways. Tidal sluices filled the baths and as a child he had feared what the inrush might bring. Crabs and jellyfish and eels. One night he saw the girl swimming there. She wore a rubber cap and a one-piece bathing costume with a cuff that reached an inch down her thighs such as swimmers in the thirties and forties might have worn. As she walked to the edge of the diving board he could see that she was pregnant.

She dived cleanly from the board and he watched as she swam lengths in the dusk, passing up and down over the moray-prowled dark.

On long continental runs he had started to hear ghostly tappings from the container behind his cab. He thought he could hear cries.

She swam on into October. Through the neap tides. Wrack piled against the seaward wall of the baths. She looked sleek and otterish in the briny pool, heavy when she hauled herself out, streaming water, heavy-pelted. There was foul weather in the deep-sea fishing grounds and the trawlers were tied up. The rust-streaked hulls and dented plating of the ageing fleet brought an uneasy awareness of tumultuous seas and fogbound banks to the silent port.

The bad weather stopped and fishing resumed. He was on the road day and night. Once when he was waiting for a load he walked up the slope behind the plant to the chalets where the women were housed. There were broken pallets and fish boxes strewn about the path. The huts were made of cracked salt planks with flat bitumen roofs. He felt as if he had stumbled upon a lost township.

One evening when she was swimming he tried to leave her passport back. He stood outside the cubicle where she had left her clothes. A loose piece of guttering rattled against the wall. His nerve failed him. He had gone too far by taking the passport in the first place. He realised that he might be only one of a range of figures of shadowy authority in her life. He wondered who these companions that he had made for himself might be. When he went out again she was still swimming lengths, the rubber swim cap's wet gleam against the dark water.

There were storms closer to home in November. A procession of Westerlies marching up the North Channel. The ferries were cancelled and the fishing fleet was tied up. The baths were closed. Gales carried silt and shingle over the railing and into the pool. Weeds caught on the railings and hung in dark swags and festoons. He still walked down on the esplanade and met her there one morning. She was wearing a cheap brown anorak from the chandlery at the harbour and rigger boots. She wore very little make-up. Her lips were chapped, her cheeks reddened with what looked like windburn. She looked like a member of a tribe—a Mongol or Tartar. Someone who had ridden in hordes across the windblown steppe.

'Not much chance to swim in this weather,' he said.

'No,' she said, 'I like to go to gym instead but...' she touched her stomach lightly. She gave no sign of having recognised him.

That night he went to the disco at the Atlantic. There was salt spray blowing across the car park. Security men in ill-fitting dinner jackets at the door. They put a stamp in ultra-violet ink on the back of your hand at the door when you paid. An otherworldly motif with which to enter the night ahead.

He went to the bar and ordered a beer. An ultraviolet disco light caught the stamp on the back of his hand. After a while he became aware of a commotion from the toilets. He went over. Through the open door he saw the pregnant girl holding on to the edge of a basin, the other hand on her stomach.

He drove her to the hospital in the rig. Four of the Russian girls climbed into the bunk behind him with her. When they got to the hospital she was put into a cubicle in accident and emergency.

'What's her name?' the nurse asked.

'Nadia Hamsa,' he said. The road wife opened her eyes and looked at him. He thought it would have been better if she had caught him returning the passport at the pool. If she had loomed over him. If she had darkened the cubicle door with her watery shadow.

The nurse pushed a clipboard across the desk to him and he filled it out. The Russian girls watched him, blonde girls with the imprint of the ultraviolet stamp on their hands. They looked as if they had been caught in the light of distant planets, as though they had fallen through the pulsing wavelengths, the cosmic stream.

The foetal heartbeat was being monitored on a screen. The line rose and fell slowly. He felt that unearthly processes were taking place. The road wife's eyes were closed. Her breathing was even. The blankets were pale, sad colours. The atmosphere in the room was such that Coyle felt he would turn around and see Death, or some attendant to Death leaning against the wall behind him, a louche, cold figure that may have been following him around for some time.

He fell asleep in the steel-framed chair. When he woke a nurse was detaching the monitor. The road wife looked up. Their eyes met again. He understood that you were only entitled to a certain amount of absolution, and that it was possible to use it up.

He left her passport at the reception desk and went out into the night. The storms had reached their peak. Shreds of plastic pallet wrap fluttered wildly from telegraph lines. In the inner harbour ships' halyards rattled against mast tines and company pennants streamed from mastheads. The armies of the night were abroad bearing pale insignia.

When he came back the next day the road wife was gone. She had discharged herself and taken the passport. She had been seen that morning getting into the cab of a Dutch registered Scania bound for Harwich. Ten days later an immigration official came to the plant to interview Coyle.

'Why do you want to talk to me?' Coyle asked.

'You ticked the box as next of kin.'

'Did I?' Not knowing what dark and self-absorbed idea of kinship had gripped him.

'Her name wasn't Hamsa by the way. That passport was stolen last year in Dover.'

For a few weeks he drove a ten-tonner on the early run to the airport. He delivered live prawns crated and boxed for air freight to the Far East. Afterwards he would park along the boundary fence and watch the planes take off in the dark, the van rocked with jetwash. He envisaged the prawns seventy thousand feet up in the pressurised holds, their tiny antennae probing the night.

She was gone and others were taking her place. From the frost haunted cities of the north. From the mountainous republics. Populations in movement, streaming through the air hubs and the ferry ports. He thought that if he lasted until spring and went back to the swimming baths he might find her poised on the high board in her old-fashioned swimming costume and rubber cap like a phantom Olympian.

He joined the other workers to watch martial arts films in the evening. Thinking that he might see a rustling hostess in silk moving silently in the background. Thinking of faces he might glimpse in the triad-haunted narrow streets, abroad in the night with the deadly yakuza. He drove night freight to Bremen, Rotterdam, Gdansk. The great northern ports. Not knowing if the day would come when he would be called upon to open a container door upon a dead Chinese family. Ageless, dynastic figurines crouched in the dark like tomb gifts.

Storm Glass

Kathleen Murray

The Shortlist Citation

A stylish, remarkably confident story that makes a pretty
virtue out of the flecks of stark memory and language with
which we construct a cohesive past and a saving view of
ourselves within it. Narratively, it is a rich and moving
variation upon an image—storm—the radiant consequences
of which last on far beyond its appointed day.

—Richard Ford

Author's note:

A few years ago a friend phoned telling me to switch on the radio to hear a documentary about a storm in Kilkee. I rang my father to tell him because that was his home place; he said he remembered that very storm. We both hung up to listen to the programme and never talked about it again.

The storm idea kicked off the story and then it went down a few roads. At one stage it was about a man who was involved in showbands but that proved not to be the case. When I wrote this story, I was thinking about how we live out the story of our lives in relation to each other.

In 'Storm Glass' stories are used to stitch together the fragments of past and work a way into the future. Things that seemed fixed and real at one stage of life—dogs in hats, clocks, notions about people—have eroded with time; tales shore up the memories, sandbags of words. The stories are as true as the characters here can muster and still behind them are the shadows of stories that are not being told for whatever reasons.

— *Kathleen Murray*

My husband peels an orange and clears off the pith with his thumbnail. He does this without looking at his hands. He places the peel in the paper bag on the handbrake between us.

'This,' he says, 'I'd say, might be the tastiest orange I've ever eaten.'

He tells me about the orange because I am sitting there beside him in the car.

'You know what keeps me going?' he says. 'The notion that before I die I might eat another orange that'll be even sweeter. Or I'll wake up after a great sleep to a perfect mug of coffee. That's what's keeping me going right now. Not who steps off that boat or who might turn up on our doorstep. Not even meeting up in the afterlife. I've let that go too.'

'You want to know what's keeping me going?' I say. 'The notion that maybe we're being watched while we're sitting here doing the watching.'

For the past two years we set out every Sunday to go to our favourite spot in the car park to the right of the ferry dock. I bring soup in a flask, soup I make on Saturday evenings, bread, fruit, sometimes a small bottle of wine to share. We have the

Sunday papers propped up on the dashboard. Right before we drive home we open the doors and get out and standing beside the car, we stretch our legs, flex our neck muscles. You can't see much more standing up.

A ferry goes to the two islands three times a day and we like to be there for all three crossings. In the winter the service drops back to twice a day. You can pick out the tourists from the locals heading over and back to the main island. We both watch for people from the smaller island; we know most of their faces now, although the shaved heads and robes made it difficult at first.

My father was dozing when I called.

'I was just listening to the radio,' he said. 'There was a documentary on, about a storm, 1951 it was, all along the western seaboard.'

Since Mother died two years ago he has become more talkative on the phone.

'Edmond Carmody was interviewed,' he continued, 'though he was only a child then. We were in the same class in school and then up training in the Park together. He got posted down to Cork and I stayed in Dublin. He was Assistant Police Commissioner by the time he retired.'

'You should get in touch with him.'

'Why would I do that? He's had a heart condition for years and the wife was nearly completely blind. Diabetes. Did he have a stroke? Maybe it was she had the stroke.'

'Well, he'd probably enjoy the chance to reminisce. I could drive you there sometime.'

'Ah I don't think so. I'm too tired. He never took his health seriously even when he was in the Force and your health is everything, everything. The Carmodys owned the Lighthouse Hotel, years back it catered for the upper echelons. The seaweed baths were very popular with the English at one stage. Skin conditions particularly. Later it got very popular with the Christian Brothers. Edmond and I, we'd run errands for them, get them cream or cigarettes. For a few bob.'

'Ice creams?'

'Ah no, skin creams. They came for the baths, they often had skin conditions and they weren't used to the sun. Edmond had to sweep the seats of the chairs after their meals, with all the white flakes; it was like a snow storm, a skin storm. He had it hard. He never mentioned about his mother on the radio. John Finnegan the porter, he was the last one to see her alive. He said he was chatting to her in the lobby as the band was finishing up that Saturday night. It was thought she might have gone to check on her maiden aunt up the strand line. The sea wall collapsed and she was taken out to sea. '

'Was the body ever found?'

'No, but a few weeks later, bright day for the end of January, the weather was off the scale that year, her shoes were found by visitors, a honeymoon couple, up on Marsh's Head, placed together behind the ditch. We all waited and watched to see if a body would surface and the boats went out to caves where bodies had turned up before. They found one, a child from up the coast who had gone over fishing, but there was never any sighting of Mrs Carmody. It split that family, with the husband thinking it was a freak wave and the rest thinking it was herself.'

'What difference how she ended up in the sea at the end of the day?'

'Well, it seemed to make every difference to the children, the daughters especially. I was only pally with Edmond. The first boy, Michael, joined the Army. But the girls took against the father for some reason and they never darkened his door after they left home. All bar the littlest one, Maura. You probably remember her, she was always going up and down the strand line with a small dog, and she would have a straw hat on him.'

'I don't remember that dog.'

'Maybe it wasn't you, but one of you children, maybe it was Brian, was mad about that dog. King Charles Spaniel. I was sure it was you. She'd feed it an ice cream cone every day. She ran the hotel but she was eccentric. Ran it into the ground eventually. No, now I don't think it was you. It was Brian. Two of the Carmody girls went out to Australia nursing and one was a nun in Venezuela, or was it Peru? Where is the Angel Falls on the border of? She sent me a mass card when your mother died. Most unusual depiction of the Crucifixion on the card, I think the waterfall was in the background.'

I hoped he couldn't hear me cleaning out the fridge, opening the compost bin quietly to deposit rotting cucumbers and chillies while he recalled the wind that caused the sea to climb over the sea wall and travel well beyond, fifty-foot breakers smashing the newly built esplanade. Seawater flooding his mother's front parlour; furniture floating on the main street; barometers behaving erratically. The beach turned over many times in the night forming strange contours, sand castles of a giant fingerless child.

The fridge door, once the gallery of potato prints and crayoned drawings, is now covered with her cards. Our daughter sends us unusual postcards from the island, with unintelligible messages, familiar words in unfamiliar configurations from a plane of higher enlightenment.

'It's the next Waco, that's what we're looking at here,' my husband says to me and to anyone else who is stationary in front of him; waiters, neighbours, taxi drivers.

If I could send Grace a message it would be no more sophisticated than those parents who appear in the news flanked by police officers saying, 'Please come home, we just want our daughter back.' Pleas from the parent of a small child abducted, not the mother of a young woman who has chosen to become invisible.

I am writing a story for my daughter Grace: *Once upon a time there was a storm in a seaside town.* I want to tell her the story as if it were a childish adventure in the lives of her grandparents, lives that were as idyllic as was possible in 1950s Ireland with a war over and none able to imagine the troubles ahead.

The story could begin with a conversation taking place along the esplanade of some seaside town when they were courting or on one of their first holidays together. Sitting on a towel drinking tea from a flask, my father drying himself off after a swim, taking a moment in the sun before they had to get a train back to Dublin. The waves meeting the rocks breaking the memory of the storm of 1951, arriving with the quality of a dream remembered hours later, fully intact. He tells my mother, not yet a mother, of flounder trapped under roof tiles, lobster pots found three fields away, the band above in Carmody's Lighthouse Hotel that performed 'Stormy Weather' four times that night in their set. She then tells him of the sheep stranded on high ground in snow drifts, her father and brother tethered together going out to settle the horses, the sycamore tree torn from the earth, blocking the path to the well; she tells him of a crow that danced all night on the wind, plunging through sheets of snow towards her bedroom window.

I want to think they talked about this during their courtship and not a few years later, after they were married. Because then my father might have added in some other memories of that winter. December 1951 was also when his brother Patsy tied himself to a chair at the range and refused to go back to the boarding school after Christmas and he bit their mother, drawing blood from her wrist. Eventually they got him dressed and in the cart with his feet and hands tied until they were hours away from home. He was broken then and they untied him. If he told my mother this part of the story of the storm, she would be silent for a few moments, sifting this new knowledge into the adult Patsy she knew: alcoholic, schizophrenic. The story would have shifted from the storm and left them with the thought of Patsy, a twelve-year-old boy trussed like a pig, forced to return to whatever troubles school held for him.

Maybe they talked about the storm for the first time years later the night of December 23rd 1975, when they got a phone call to say Patsy and a friend had come down in a light aircraft. We were housebound because of the icy roads and my head was filled with bicycles, the likelihood of a racer, the challenge of getting the wheels down our chimney. My brother Brian spent the evening on his knees, not as mother thought praying for Patsy but making a last-minute intercession for the safe arrival of Action Man and his helicopter. While my parents waited for more information and wondered what had taken Patsy up in a plane on a night like that, they passed the time telling each other of odd seasons and storms, maybe recalling 1951 for the first time. Nine days he survived in the hospital with a broken spine before dying on the first day of 1976. His death was fractured, stretching across two years, seeing out the old and bringing in the new.

The date of the storm—December 27th 1951—just after Christmas Day, before the New Year, lessening its chance of staking a claim on their memory: to be overtaken by the first Christmas together as husband and wife; Aunt May's fall on New Years Eve; the year Brian's head was caught in the bannisters; Patsy's accident; to be overtaken by stories that belonged to my parents together, our family stories.

My mother, ten years old in 1951, lived in the hill country and never having seen the sea spent the night of the storm lying in bed next to her sister worrying about sheep. As her father's numb hands forced their way into mittens she worked her mind into the body of a sheep, trying to decide where was best to go for shelter and what the sheep would do to survive. Come back to the yard, she willed, or even the trees at the top of the track, but to go towards the sheds would risk full-scale assault by the wind. The sheets of rain and sleet turning into snow were blinding, too easy to lose your bearing. She got on her knees and prayed before the cold drove her back into bed.

My father, at the other side of the country, marvelled at random acts he couldn't understand—how a storm managed to destroy some buildings and leave others untouched. Odd objects were recovered from the beach the day after, a crutch, a milk churn, a school desk, a ship's wheel, things that should have been one place turned up in another.

My mother's lasting memory is of the next morning when she pulled back the curtain, the covering of snow, the mass of sheep bleating in one low voice and she believed for these first few moment that they were all there, each one had survived the night. She wasn't party to the culling of the maimed animals that were stranded in out-of-the-way corners, the broken limbs, a couple of lambs born that night too early at their mother's side, glassy eyes waiting in the white stillness, death coming slowly then quickly. The crow, it must not have been right in the head, dropping so low, flapping madly and swooping up to cover her window, black wings fanning out. She wondered how a living creature could enjoy that chaos without fear for life or limb.

I think they never put these scenes together, my mother and father, in all their years of talk. It's a shame. It would have made her laugh: the thought of him sweeping eels up the main street while she was counting lambs, hoping that her will might fasten them to safety through the night.

Maybe they talked about the storm after my father gave up the drink properly for the last time and they were attending the counsellor together. He might have told her a more truthful version then, that it was he, not Patsy, tied to the cart returning to school. Patsy never went to secondary school, he was too wild. My father believed the storm was an act of God, his deliver me from evil. When he woke up on the 28th of December he thought he would not have to return, that he would be let stay home with Grandmother to clear up the damage to the shop and eventually the idea of school would fade until he became a permanent fixture behind the counter, measuring flour, carrying in deliveries. In the evenings he would eat dinner with her, then go off fishing with the boys down at the pier or practising his dives off the boards in Diamond Bay. His heart expanded that morning, hearing the talk about the collapsed esplanade and the boats destroyed and the electricity cut off. He checked the storm glass in the front parlour; it confirmed the weather as *stormy*. In my father's mind that teak banjo played 'Stormy Weather' all afternoon. He had a whole two days of belief before she took his uniform out to wash and press.

After the phone call with my father I wondered about the shoes; if Mrs Carmody, thinking her husband would forgo new shoes for the girls, had meant them to be found and now at least one of them would have a decent pair. The next time I spoke to Father I asked him.

'I can tell you one thing, we valued our footwear then,' he said. 'I'd say that's why her shoes were left there; she wouldn't want them marked by the salt or dashed on the rocks below.'

In truth Mrs Carmody was taken with walking barefoot; she wanted to take that last short walk without shoes. She enjoyed the feel of the hotel carpet on the soles of her feet although this was a source of annoyance to her husband. He did not allow her paddle in the warm tidal pools with the children, had censured her for removing her shoes on an autumn day when they picked damsons. The pair of shoes was a last gesture, an act of defiance he could not prevent, a final note from his wife.

There were people from all over the town stretched out along the beach the morning after the storm with flour sacks and grain bags, some even with their pillowcases. They were filling them with sand and bringing them back home on handcarts for fear of further flooding. The Carmody children worked alongside the rest, stomachs tightening with breakfasts that had never appeared. Late afternoon, only then would their father allow the alarm to be raised, but the clouds were low and it was too dark to organise a search for their mother that evening.

Weeks later when the shoes were found Bernadette, the eldest of the Carmody girls, became convinced that her mother had not died the night of the storm. She believed Mrs Carmody was watching the guests leave the hotel throughout the day from a hiding place on the cliff. Waiting up there, waiting for a sign that someone had been sent to look for her. Bernadette was haunted by this notion, that their mother saw them on the beach, that she was able to pick them out, working away as if nothing untoward had happened in their home. How it would have hurt her to see her beloved son Edmond, helping his father lift the heavy bags onto the cart and the two younger girls sidling up to some older women who had food. Worst of all they had joined the other children on the beach chasing around the carcass of a whale that had washed up, screeching with the gulls. Throughout the summer of 1952 Bernadette made the other children try it themselves: one child climbing up the cliff to the spot where the shoes were found and the others on the beach below mingling with the holiday-makers. Whether the child on the cliff could distinguish their brother and sisters from the other figures depended on who was doing the looking and who was doing the telling.

When Edmond was above he told Bernadette flat out, 'I've seen ye a mile away, each and every one. Mother must've been watching us all that day.'

But when Bernadette was above she thought she might have been able to pick Edmond out but not the younger two girls. She was more persistent than him, repeating the ritual daily. On occasions she insisted the younger girls wear the heavy winter coats they wore the day after the storm and trudge back and forth in the sunshine. Then Bernadette began to question her own eyesight and insisted she be taken into the town for an eye examination. So the doubt lingered in their minds that what drove their mother to her death was the sight of everyday life continuing on without her, watching her children on the beach while she might have been dying or thinking of death.

It was the eldest brother Michael who returned home the following Christmas on leave, the one child who was not present the night of the storm or even in the search parties after, it was Michael's version of events that held.

'Father sent her off, probably on some fool's errand. She must have decided to stay out to punish him and she was overtaken by the storm and was pushed over the edge with the wind.'

Thus their father had some blame laid at his door and the mother's own actions accounted for the rest. There was little sympathy to go around in those times so the children were expected to get on with life and they did, as best they could. One by one they moved out of the orbit of Mr Carmody taking their heaviness with them to Peru and the U.S. and a hospital and a school and a war, bar the youngest, Maura, who stayed with him after he remarried and eventually took over the hotel, running it into the ground.

*

I usually rang Brian in his office on Monday. He had a type of financial job that was always slow on Mondays. Since Mother died he collected our father and took him to his house every Sunday for dinner. They would sit on the couch for the afternoon watching football, children barrelling in and out of doors, tripping over the old man's legs, falling asleep in his lap.

'So,' he said, 'How was your weekend?'

'Fine, we drove out to the lake. How was Dad?'

'Good form, we didn't get to see the second match. He was full of chat about Carmody, his old pal from the guards. I met the sister once, you know. She taught in a school outside Waterford, Sister Bernadette.'

'Was she not out on the missions?'

'No, it was her sister the nurse who went out to Peru. You know Bernadette went to secretarial college with Mam before she had her vocation. I brought Mam to visit her once; it was her golden jubilee or something like that. We were treated like a couple of foreign dignitaries.'

Little wonder. Mother had been sending donations to the convent for years. We both remembered the weekly trips to the post office, queuing up to get the money orders. Sometimes if she was particularly agitated she would just stuff some pound notes into an envelope with the intercession scribbled out on a sheet of writing paper. Any money she could get her hands on, it became a compulsion, bill money and clothes money and our pocket money sent to change the direction of her life, to bring all the lost sheep home.

'You don't remember a dog wearing a hat when we were kids?' I asked.

'No. It sounds more like your kind of thing. I do remember a donkey wearing a necklace that bit my foot. Do you remember that? Any news from Gracie?'

'No.'

'Well, give her time.'

I want to halt Grace's life story back when she was still eating the food we put on her plate, still ordering burgers and milkshakes when we went out. Then to skip ahead, past the part where she became obsessed with her skin and cleanliness and her nails and her hair and cutting them shorter and shorter until her fingers and scalp bled. Past the part that led her to a commune in London, fasting, fasting all the time and washing her clothes and hair and fingers in cold dirty water. Past the compound in Western Scotland, all contact with us denied. And now back here, on the island. I'll skip to the part in the future where she has already come back to us. Beyond the moments of return because they will be joyous and painful and difficult, to a time when she is back right here in the city, living in her own apartment and she calls me the night of a storm. She wants to check on us because she is our only daughter and we her only parents. She wants to draw our attention to the warnings on the radio about power cuts. Have we got candles and torches and a flask filled with hot water? She will be calm listening to her father describing the neighbours' new boat parked in their front drive. When I tell her about her grandfather and my clinics she seems distracted but only because there is a TV on in the background not because of contrary thought streams in her head and she is going to see us that weekend anyway.

'I have to go, Mam. Don't forget to switch everything off if the power goes. See you Sunday.'

We are already prepared ever since the major power blackout back in 2003. But Grace missed that, inside her cocoon at that time, barely aware of dawn and dusk, never mind approaching fronts from the Atlantic or hurricanes gathering momentum over Cuba. So we are prepared.

Did every family own a barometer? I meant to ask my father but the conversation had moved on and I forgot. My father inherited his barometer from the family home and passed it on to me. The gradations astonished us as children, how this instrument knew a cloudy from a sunny day, could tell stormy from dry. These words seemed too vague and slightly unbelievable, nothing like the absolute measurements of the clock where half past two was half past two. The hands moved to tell exactly the time, minute by minute, tick by tock, constantly keeping up with the present. Time had no personal qualities; back then we accepted the passing of time, the immutability of numbers without a thought. But the storm glass, it had the personality of a cantankerous old man who studies the sleeping posture of cows or the rings around the moon before pronouncing the weather. It was only my father who said storm glass, my mother taught us the correct phrase, barometer. When we were a little older we would try and catch him out, pointing to the barometer indicating *Fair* when it was raining outside.

'Long foretold—long last, short notice—soon past,' he would always respond. 'But not forever, nothing is forever, particularly the weather.'

The Rescue

Susan Stairs

The Shortlist Citation

A nervy, tightly-compressed, and alarmingly brief story of human extremis: children hurtling to the ends of the too-short tethers connecting them to modern existence. Graceful and knowing in its stripped-out and plumbed bleakness, it is a love story—of a kind—but a kind in which love scarcely avails.

—**Richard Ford**

Author's note:

A boy. A girl. A bedroom. A weapon. This is what I had when I started to write 'The Rescue'. The story went through many transformations and edits before it finally became what it is, but this potentially explosive mix of four ingredients did not change. I held them close and tried to weave as tight a narrative as possible around them, curious to see what would happen as a result.

I chose each word carefully and consciously, determined that the story's brevity should not hinder its breadth. The opening paragraph is deliberately ambiguous, and while I don't expect that by the end of the story it all 'makes sense' to the reader, I did want to engender a confusion, a tension, that might slowly result in some sort of clarity as the narrative progresses.

'The Rescue' is fundamentally about boundaries, the consequences of the lack of them and the intrinsic desire of human beings to create them. It is about the basic need we all have to feel safe, to feel tied to something, to connect. It is also about expectations; those we have of others, and those we have of ourselves.

— *Susan Stairs*

HE'S IN. THE PUSH was easy. Though it's the first time, it's familiar. The smell excites. Like birth and death, cut and cure. The good and bad of everything in equal measure. How it should be. He pants like a beast in the black, insides heaving with dread and command. And her. Slivers of her scent urge him to explore. Tearing through limbs of rooms, surfaces sleek and coarse and papery against his fingers. Steps of silent air under his feet. A savage chiming in his head.

He likes the word 'Private'. Red letters on the door of her room. Private means you don't have to explain. He thinks he might tippex it onto the stainless-steel blade of the boning knife he carries in his schoolbag. The door handle twists. The floor turns blue. The walls jerk with dark-eyed faces laid flat against leaves of pink and gold. Another threshold crossed. He feels behind, pushes the door half closed. In its lock, the silver key taunts. He yanks it, thrusts it into his trouser pocket.

Shauna swings down Stoneycourt Drive, takes her time. It's Friday afternoon. Nothing means so much that she has to rush. And the sweet deliciousness of an empty house has long since lost its appeal. She can do without most things, if it comes down to it.

Rain starts, waves her black hair, soaks her unsuitable shoes, slides off the navy raincoat draped over her arm. Her green gaze searches the pavement, familiar cracks and tar lines criss-crossing her route, like the marks she scores on the winter-white skin of her arms with a compass point.

She kicks an empty Coke bottle. It spins as it skitters across the deserted road and down the Mullens' drive, lodging against the back wheel of their shiny Mercedes. Katie Mullen's such a bitch. All that pouting and posing and fluffing up her hair. And the way she laughs at everything Mr. Horan says in class. Even when he's not trying to be funny.

Katie's home already, chauffeured by her mother. Heated leather seats and cup holders for her Starbucks. It's all did-you-get-much-homework-and-what-would-you-like-for-your-dinner-Katie? Everything smooth. So much comfort, it's like a religion. The Mullens are the kind of people you hope things will go wrong for.

Katie and Shauna used to be best friends. Sat together from the first day of school. All the way up: playdates and sleepovers and secret diaries. But the start of secondary heralded the end of it all. New girls in shiny wrappers, like chocolates to choose from. And Katie sampled all flavours. Shauna is slow to soften in the mouth, difficult on the jaws. Too much effort and not quite sweet enough. The kind only the very few have a taste for.

He sweeps his hair across his forehead, dumps his bag on her bed, kneels down on the floor. He's in among the filth and fumble of her life, the discarded doings of her own survival. He doesn't know if it's how he imagined it would be, is not even sure if he planned it. Maybe he thought it up a long time ago, or perhaps it only came to him today. Everything melts together when he's in a beautiful place. Scents and sights and forms and textures. He never knows where he ends and the other stuff begins. No separation between what is and what's not. A sort of confusion he suspects he'll never make sense of. Like when he saw that war picture by Picasso on the school trip to Madrid. He knows its beauty excited him, seeped into him, made him shudder. But everything else from that time muddles the memory: the gibber of his group outside the museum, the belting blue of the sky, red wine spattered on the sheets of his hotel bed and somebody's fist in his stomach.

The window is acned with rain. Stretching out his spider legs, he lies his body flat, wonders how long he's waited for this moment. Rolling over and back across the floor, her detritus clings to his grey jumper like clues: wisps of scissor-cut hair, clips and pins and lengths of black thread, price-tags from new clothes ripped off in desire, lumps of chewed gum spat out in disgust. He screws up his eyes, blinks hard, over and over. His chest collects balls of blue fluff, mascara-smeared tissues, used cotton wool. His fingernails claw at the carpet, rising dust settling in his nostrils. Reaching under her bed, he pulls out a pair of purple canvas shoes, scribbled all over, rubber soles still smelling like new.

She wonders if she should change as soon as she gets in. Or make toast, watch TV, let her clothes dry out from the heat of her body. She might throw on her pyjamas, pour a bowl of

Cheerios, log on to Bebo. Shauna hates making decisions, would prefer if someone else made them for her. She can't stand it when people ask what she plans to do after school. How the fuck would she know. Why would she even care. Plans are boring. She prefers surprises. But sometimes even they disappoint. Like that time her father called with her present, a week after her tenth birthday. She knew it was a basketball without even unwrapping it. She wished he'd made more of an effort to disguise it.

She senses it when she walks into the hall. The stain of invasion. The unmistakable spectre of stealth. The air is not as she left it this morning. Someone has sliced through it on their way up the stairs. She dumps her stuff. Wet footprints mark her ascent, each one more faint than the last, until the top two steps register no sign at all of her climb.

Her science teacher once told her she was reckless. It was the day they were doing that experiment with hydrochloric acid, and Shauna had pulled off her Plexiglas safety goggles; she couldn't see through their scratched lenses. In English class, she'd looked up 'reckless' in the dictionary. It took ages; she thought it began with a 'W', and that it might mean she was incapable of being destroyed. 'Careless of consequences' it said when she finally found it. The explanation pleased her. She'd thanked the science teacher later, receiving Saturday detention for her gratitude.

Scrambling to his feet, he wonders how it is that he's not meant to be here. This is comfort. This is where he fits. He's heard the front door slam, the thud of steps. But there's no threat in her arrival. The breath that earlier escaped his throat in pithy, erratic spurts, now waves easy in and out of his chest. Nothing around him is clear. He hears the gold leaves whispering on the wall, feels the rain pricking his face. He rocks forward on his toes. His eyes sting. This is the parachute line. In the second before she enters the room, he lurches behind the door, melting his flesh and bone into the prism of the space, waiting, until he's sure his landing will be safe. He'll have to be quicker than real life. Cartoon-quick. He slams the door, sliding his weight against it.

One time she'd made her arms bleed, her mother had bought her the pair of purple Converse. Shauna hadn't been that pushed about them, but she knew the purchase made her mother feel better. Compared to any of the more usual forms of treatment, the shoes were just an ersatz pick-me-up. She'd marked his name six times on each one with a dark green gel pen, then tossed them under her bed with all her similarly unworn footwear. So she doesn't understand why, when he stands there with his back to her bedroom door, the only thing she can think of to say is:

'What the fuck are you doing with my Converse, Evan?'

The shoes are tucked under his left arm. He pulls them out, dangling them by their pink laces right in front of his face.

'You've written my name all over them.'

'That was ages ago. It's over, Evan. Now get the hell out of my room, please. My mother'll be home soon.'

He wipes his tongue over his teeth.

'She's away for the weekend with her new boyfriend again,' he says. 'Everyone knows that, Shauna.' He shows her his best smile. 'It's just you and me.'

She stares at him.

The first time they'd kissed, she'd kept her eyes wide open. It was only partly so she could make out Katie Mullen's reaction. There was something about Evan that wasn't quite real. As if he might turn into a wild beast if you didn't hold his gaze.

'Come away from the door, Evan. You're not funny.'

'You never answer my texts. I thought we were friends.'

'For fuck's sake! You went off with that bitch!'

He drops the shoes to the floor, wonders what it will take.

'I dreamed about you last night.'

'Evan. Please go,' she sighs. 'I need to put on dry clothes. This is just too weird. I can't believe you actually broke into my house.'

'I hate her too, you know.'

She leans in towards him, narrows her eyes, picks a pearl-headed pin from his sleeve, notices all the stuff on his jumper.

'Were you lying on my floor? What the hell? What's wrong with you?'

He didn't think she'd be so close so soon. Under his arms he's hot and itchy, and the skin on his scalp crawls, the way it did when he thought he'd caught head lice from that chubby, asthmatic boy he sat beside in fourth class.

'I want to show you something,' he tells her.

She wades through the mess on her floor, sits down on her unmade bed, wonders if this'll be anything like the time of the Angel Tattoo, which had made her realise—much too late, of course—that she really should pay far more attention. Her curiosity, as usual, is only mildly aroused, and with Evan, you don't expect answers to questions, at least not to the ones you've asked. So she sits there, waiting for his revelation.

It's getting dark. A kind of gelatinous murk has infiltrated the air in her room, making it seem like she's looking at him through the science class safety goggles. She could turn on her bedside lamp, but that would spoil it all. Despite her protestations, she's enjoying this scenario. And who knows the damage forty-watts might do. He's made such an effort, broken into her house, ignored the red letters on her door. What's not to admire. And he's still as cute as he ever was. She wants to text Katie Mullen right now, let her know he's here in her bedroom. But her phone's in the pocket of her raincoat, lying in a heap on the hall floor.

'Open the side part of my bag,' he says in a cracked whisper.

'What? Speak up, Evan my boy!' she says in mock command, judge to witness. She giggles, hopes he's smiling at her across the dusky space.

'The side pocket. Open it,' he says, louder this time. 'And kind of pull the zipper to the right, or it'll keep getting stuck.'

It was a lucid dream that Evan had last night. The best kind. Shauna wasn't in it by chance. He placed her there as soon as he understood he was dreaming. She was locked in a wooden chest in the attic of a house just like this one. At least, it looked like this one from the outside. Inside, it was a puzzle-book confusion of post-TV-makeover rooms: spacious and spectral with show-off curtains, fully set dining tables and pale, painted floorboards. At the outset, his task appeared simple—to run to the top of the house and release her. But the rooms grew dense with a milling crowd, walking in circles, standing in his way, blocking his progress. Doors were locked, steps led nowhere, rooms divided and multiplied. He tried to relate the urgency of his quest to those around him, but they either wouldn't listen or couldn't understand his words. As time passed in a panic of chatter and punches and flashing lights, he could see her lying in her dark box, mouldering away, humming softly, while the skin fell in bloody strips from her thin, putrid arms.

And he was the only one who knew where she was.

'What is it?' Shauna asks.

'Just take it out,' he tells her.

The knife is carefully wrapped in Evan's school scarf. She unrolls the navy and grey stripes.

'What do those words mean?' She turns her head to read the Latin inscription under the embroidered school crest. He's impatient.

'Drop it onto the bed,' he says. 'Don't handle it.'

'It says… Deus… something… something. Deus has to do with religion, doesn't it? I think it might mean…' the knife plops out 'God… God! Oh my God! What the fuck, Evan?'

Even in the light-starved room, the blade manages to flash. Shauna looks at it lying against her grubby lilac sheet, can't take her eyes away from it.

'What do you think?' he asks. Waiting for her reply, he turns and quietly locks the door, replaces the key in his pocket, moves across the floor towards her.

She holds her breath high in her chest. The point of the knife is as perfect as anything could be.

'It's so clean,' she says. 'It's just right.'

He's down on his knees beside her, resting his head on her thigh, his heat seeping through to her flesh.

'You know I'm sorry about the Katie thing,' he whispers into her damp skirt. 'That night... I don't know....she just kept at me. It wasn't what I wanted. Things happen all the time that I don't want.'

She lets her fingers creep through his dark hair.

'Did you want this?'

'I don't know... I mean... yeah, I want to be here now. But I think this just happened too. He lifts his head to look at her. 'I'm so sorry if I scared you.'

'I think I knew you were here,' she says. 'And nothing much scares me anyway. You know that.'

She shifts across the bed and they lie down. He takes the knife, places it on his stomach. She feels his breath on her cheek, his face close enough for her to make out the crimson pinpricks of a young bruise.

'Did it happen again?' she wants to know

'You should take off your clothes. You're all damp.'

'Why do you let them, Evan?'

He fits his hand inside the collar of her shirt.

'You're all damp,' he says again. He helps her pull her jumper over her head.

'Don't you care?' she asks. 'Don't they make you want to kill them?'

He spreads her hair out over the pillow. 'It's hard to hurt with your bare hands.'

They lie in the grey silence. Rain falls harder on the roof tiles, drips, staccato-like, into the down-pipe outside the window. Shauna smiles to herself. She knows it's going to happen. They'd talked about it before the Katie thing, back when they'd seen each other every day for weeks. She wouldn't share such a secret thing with anyone else. He's undoing her shirt buttons now. Short shocks of freezing fingertips on her clammy skin. She believes so much in this. Believes in it because there's nothing else that fires her. Hungry afternoons slurring into hollow evenings, with no questions to answer. And no comfort to measure the pain.

'What happened in your dream?' she asks.

'Nothing much.' He laughs. 'You were trapped, I had to rescue you. That's about it.'

'And did you?'

He sits up to tug off his shirt and jumper.

'Of course I did.'

They turn in to each other. She reads her name under the angel on his shoulder and realises she knew all along he'd come back. She tastes the acrid fix of tobacco on the back of his tongue, likes the way his teeth don't hesitate but his eyes feel the need to be gentle.

'It won't hurt too much?' he wants to know.

She reaches down her side of the bed. 'This'll help.'

They drink from the bottle of Smirnoff in turns.

Now it gets deeper and the usual mix-up begins. He holds her wrist—wraith-like—as if it belongs to someone like her. The after-school punch comes alive on his cheek, layers of skin galloping towards the yellow and blue of tomorrow. This pain will be different. For both of them. This is a choosing, a convulsive discipline aching to discharge.

'This is just us, isn't it?' he asks.

'Just us,' she says, handing him the knife. 'In private.'

It's almost too sharp. Just the tip is all it takes, scarcely scoring, barely breaking through. Easy. And the blood. The proof. Sheets splattered again on a beautiful day. He's so sure of the good that will come from this. The healing from the wounding. The curing from the cut. She lies still for a moment, relishing the familiar: the breath in, the blood out. He watches how she takes the blade from his hand, lies his arm across her ribs, feels for the inside softness. She teases first, like skimming stones on water. Flickering, lullaby strokes that excite but don't achieve. Then she pushes and his skin yields.

He knows now why he came. It all makes sense, is clearer, neater. She drops the deadened blade to the floor. They hold their arms up. In the almost-darkness, the spots of blood show black against their silvery skin.

'Was it okay?' Shauna wants to know. 'As good as I said?'

He nods.

'I need the bathroom,' she says.

'I locked the door. I thought that was the way it should be. Key's in my pocket.'

She straddles his thighs, reaches in, her knuckles grazing the angle of his hipbone.

'You're right,' she says. 'This is the way it should be.'

Sliding off him, she opens the window, flings the key out into the rain.

'Someone will come to the rescue,' she whispers into the comfort of his mouth. 'They have to. Just like you did in your dream.'

Notes on the Authors

Richard Ford was born in Jackson, Mississippi, in 1944. He is the author of nine volumes of fiction, including three books of stories and six novels. He is the editor of *The Granta Book of the American Short Story Volumes I and II*, and is a frequent contributor of *The New Yorker* magazine. He has won the PEN-Malamud Prize for distinguished contributions to the short story. His trilogy of novels, *The Sportswriter, Independence Day* and *The Lay of the Land* are published by Bloomsbury.

Claire Keegan was raised on a farm in Wicklow. The stories from her collections, *Antarctica* and *Walk The Blue Fields* (Faber & Faber) have won several awards including The William Trevor Prize, The Edge Hill Prize, The Tom Gallon Award, The Olive Cook Award, The Rooney Prize for Irish Literature, The Hugh Leonard Bursary, the Macaulay Fellowship and The Francis MacManus Award. She also teaches creative writing. A member of Aosdána, she lives in rural Ireland.

Mary Leland is a Cork-born journalist. She has published two novels *The Killeen* (1985) and *Approaching Priests* (1991) and a book of short stories, *The Little Galloway Girls* (1986/87). Other short stories have appeared in several Irish and UK anthologies and she has also published *The Lie of the Land: Journeys through Literary Cork* (1999), *That Endless Adventure: a History of the Cork Harbour Commissioners* (2001) and *Dwyers of Cork: A Family Business and a Business Family* (2008).

Molly McCloskey is the author of two collections of short stories—*Solomon's Seal* and *The Beautiful Changes*—and a novel, *Protection*. She has won several awards for her short stories, including the RTE Francis MacManus Award. She is currently completing a non-fiction account concerning schizophrenia within her family. She was born in Philadelphia in 1964 and came to Ireland in 1989, where she has lived ever since.

Eoin McNamee was born in Kilkeel, County Down, in 1961. His first book, the novella *The Last of Deeds*, was shortlisted for the Irish Times Literature Prize. His novels include *Resurrection Man* (1996), *The Blue Tango* (2001), *The Ultras* (2004) and *12:23* (2007). Other publications include *The Language of Birds* (poetry), two screenplays—*Resurrection Man* (1998) and *I Want You* (1998)—and four books for children. He also writes under the name John Creed. He lives in County Sligo.

Kathleen Murray is from Carlow. She lives in Dublin where she works as a researcher. Her stories have appeared in the anthologies *The Incredible Hides in Every House* and *These Are Our Lives* and in *The Stinging Fly*. She was the winner of the Fish Short Story Prize 2006/07 and is working on her first collection of short stories.

Susan Stairs lives in Dublin and has recently completed an MA in Creative Writing at UCD. She is a gradute of NCAD and has written extensively about Irish art, her most notable publications being *Markey Robinson—A Life*; *The Irish Figurists*; and *Drawing from Memory*, a biography of the Belfast artist Gladys Maccabe M.B.E. Her work has been broadcast on Sunday Miscellany on RTE Radio 1 and her short story 'Leaving Traces' features in the recent publication *A Curious Impulse*, New Writing from the MA in Creative Writing UCD 2009. She is currently working on a novel, and also writing some new short stories.

Acknowledgements

Many thanks to Redmond Doran and the Doran family for their very generous sponsorship of the Davy Byrnes Irish Writing Award. Thanks also to Gerry Smyth and Caroline Walsh of The Irish Times for their guidance and support throughout the project.

Katie Holmes handled the entries as they arrived and helped to oversee the logistics of getting them read. Our panel of readers (Philip Bellew, Robbie Brennan, Niall Byrne, Michael G. Cronin, Fiona Dunne, Francesca Lalor, Paul Leyden, Brendan Mac Evilly, Tom Mathews and Sean O'Reilly) helped to make the daunting task of reading eight hundred stories a lively and at times illuminating experience. It was an honour and a privilege to have Richard Ford as the final adjudicator. We owe him a debt of gratitude for the time and care he took in his deliberations.

Thanks to Fergal Condon for the cover; to Emily Firetog for all her work in getting this book ready for publication; and finally to the six writers for the gift of these stories.

Declan Meade
Publisher & Competition Administrator